Other books by Layne Walker
Available at amazon.com

## Action Adventure Novels
Escaping Yellowstone

## Fantasy Adventure Novels
Tainted Gold
Convergence of Time
Time Hackers

## Short Story Collection
Gold Balls of Fur and Other Snapshots of Life

Visit Layne's website at
www.laynewalkerbooks.com

# Funny Feelings

## Layne Walker

Wild Mustangs Publishing, LLC

# Funny Feelings

This is a work of fiction.
All characters and incidents are a product
of the author's imagination.
Any relationship to persons living or dead
is purely coincidental.

ISBN-13: 978-0-9883534-6-6

Cover design by
Layne Walker

Published by
Wild Mustangs Publishing, LLC
Lake Havasu City, AZ

Printing history
First edition published in November, 2018

Visit Layne's website at
www.laynewalkerbooks.com

Many thanks to Anne Cote for her hard work critiquing, editing and reshaping this novel. Without her, this book would still be in the draft stage.

# Funny Feelings

# Chapter 1

Lake Havasu City, AZ

I had my left arm draped across Chrissy's flat stomach as we lay on my couch watching a movie. Which, by the way, was one of my favorite ways of spending a hot Sunday afternoon in early September with my girlfriend.

"Hey, sweetie," I whispered into her auburn hair, "can you stop rubbing my hand? It's distracting me."

"I would," she said, sounding irritated, "but I'm not rubbing your hand. Be quiet and watch the movie."

"Come on, I can feel it. You're still doing it."

She sat up and turned to face me. Piercing blue eyes bore into mine. Holding up both hands, she said, "Does it look like I'm touching you, Brad?" She lay back down and snuggled close to me again. "Watch the movie. The good part is coming up."

Obviously, she wasn't rubbing my hand. So why did it feel like she was? I leaned across her, picked up the remote from the glass-topped coffee table, and paused the movie.

As we both sat up, Chrissy tossed back her shoulder-length hair and gave me a dirty look.

I massaged the top of my left hand, stood up, and walked across the wooden floor. Chrissy didn't say anything, but I felt her eyes on my back as I walked away.

My dog Sadie's graying, oversized scruffy ears came alert. She lifted her head from her doggie bed and watched me. Not seeing food in my hands, she went back to sleep. A mix of black lab and German shepherd, I had rescued her from a shelter two years before. I spoiled her. As a result, she was slightly overweight. If I took her outside for walks more often, she would probably lose weight, but it seemed like I was always too tired or had something else I needed to do that was more important. I made a mental note to cut back on her table scraps and snacks.

The coolness of the tile floor felt good on my bare feet as I entered the kitchen and walked to the tiled counter near the sink.

"Brad, what's going on?" Chrissy called from the other room. "Are we going to finish watching the movie or what?"

"Go ahead and start it. I'll be there in just a minute." I hated missing part of the movie, but my immediate concern was my hand. The feeling of someone rubbing it was still there and I was starting to freak out a little bit. It was like my nerves were jumping under my skin. I flipped on the florescent light over the sink and stared at the top side of my left hand. It was as though someone was lightly rubbing their fingers up and down my skin from my knuckles to my wrist.

Chrissy silently stepped up next to me. I could feel her breath over my shoulder.

I vigorously massaged the back of my hand to try to stop the strange sensation, a weirdly funny feeling.

Chrissy tucked a loose piece of her auburn hair behind her ear. "Maybe you're having an allergic reaction to something you ate."

*What had I eaten during the day? Eggs and bacon for breakfast. A burger and fries for lunch.* I shook my head.

"I don't know. I didn't eat anything out of the ordinary today."

"Your body is changing, putting on a little weight here and there." She patted my slight paunch with a grin. "Maybe you've developed an allergy to something you've always been able to eat. Maybe you're suddenly allergic to dust. Or maybe there's some kind of new pollen in the air. It could be a number of things."

Suddenly, the strange sensation disappeared. Just like that, it was gone. I lifted my hand and studied it with curiosity and relief. "Hmmm, the feeling . . . it's gone."

"Are you sure it wasn't your mind playing tricks on you?"

I shook my head. "No, I'm sure it wasn't a trick of my mind. Have you ever had anything like this happen to you? You know, some sort of funny feeling somewhere on your body?"

She shrugged her petite shoulders, the strap of her yellow top sliding down her right arm. As she replaced it, she said, "Yeah, I guess. I think people have strange sensations all the time. I'm sure I have, but I can't think of when it happened last."

"This was more than just a sensation," I replied. "It was physically real, like you . . . "

She glared at me with those baby-blue eyes, stopping me from accusing her again.

" . . . or someone else . . . like someone else was rubbing my hand." I passed my fingers across the back of my hand. "It felt so real. I've never had anything like that happen before."

Chrissy opened the cupboard. Stretching her slender five-foot-five-inch body to its limits, she plucked a bag of chips from off the top shelf. "Well it's gone now, so can we get back to the movie?"

I took one more look at my hand. "Yeah, sure." I smiled at her to ease her mind. I didn't want to ruin our

Sunday night together by letting her know how weirded-out this whole *funny feeling* thing had gotten me.

Rather than cuddle up on the couch this time, I decided to stay seated for a while and eat chips as I pondered the experience with my hand. I wanted my hand in direct sight. *I don't care what Chrissy thinks about this. What I felt wasn't just a common sensation.* I'd had plenty of sensations during my lifetime, like an irritating itch or a pulsating vein. This feeling had been different, much more immediate, more like it was coming from outside me, not inside me. The thought gave me the shivers.

While I could care less about what was going on in the movie, Chrissy seemed totally wrapped up in it. We had met six months earlier, hitting it off right away with common interests and a compelling attraction toward each other. It seemed like most nights, I visited her apartment or she came to my house. We talked about moving in together, but neither one of us was ready for that big a commitment. Not that I didn't love her, but I worked long hours during the week and interacted with a lot of people. Sometimes I wanted to have a private night to myself. Chrissy felt the same way. Deep down, I knew we'd end up getting married, but for now, this was what we both wanted and it worked well for us.

I owned a construction business called, *Brad's Handyman & Remodeling Services*. Not too original, but with a name like Brad Jones, I didn't have a lot of options. I'd thought about using my high school nickname, Jonesie, but *Jonesie's Handyman & Remodeling Services* didn't sound professional. It sounded more like a high school kid doing summer jobs, not the business of a forty-eight-year-old divorced hard-working man. For my age, I'm in pretty good shape. I'm five-nine and weigh a hundred and fifty-five pounds. I maintain a decent tan from working outside a lot, and my light brown hair is starting to show a few strands of gray. People have told me that my light blue eyes change color from blue to green, depending on my mood. *Hmmm, I hope people can't read me too closely from that.*

The movie ended without any more interruptions. Chrissy's concentrated involvement with the characters and drama had kept her attention off me. She wiped her eyes with a tissue and laughed at her own emotional response. "Well, I guess I better get going," she said. "I've got to get to work early tomorrow." As we stood up, she gave me a sweet kiss on the lips. "Thanks for the evening, Brad, and for picking out a great movie. I'll talk to you tomorrow." She picked up her purse and left.

As I watched her pull out of the driveway, I felt relieved she would not be spending the night with me. I worried I would have another weird episode and I didn't want her around to give me a hard time.

* * *

The next morning, I thought about the *funny feelings* as I drove my truck to the day's jobsite at the home of one of my repeat customers. I sighed in frustration over the memory of the feeling, still unable to explain why it happened and why it seemed so real.

When I arrived at the jobsite, the homeowner had numerous questions and concerns about the big interior painting job he'd hired me for. This was a good thing. It took my mind off the funny feelings and made me concentrate on my work.

I had a long day. By the time I got home, I was completely exhausted. I called Chrissy and told her I was too tired to get together that evening. She readily agreed because she'd had a busy day, too.

Lying in bed, it occurred to me I hadn't thought about the funny feelings since morning. And more importantly, it hadn't happened again. I chalked it up to one of those unexplainable, passing things that happen occasionally. I decided to put it out of my mind completely. As I drifted off to sleep, I thought about beautiful Chrissy and how much I enjoyed my job and being independent.

My life couldn't have been any better if I'd planned it.

# Chapter 2

Hilary Nordmeyer stormed into her husband's private room in the Whispering Pines Nursing Facility. He'd been there a week now, still in a coma from a car accident.

The short dark-skinned nurse turned to her and asked in a sugary tone. "And how are you today, Ms. Nordmeyer?"

"Tired as usual," Hilary said, annoyed at the fake friendliness of the nurse. She dropped her Gucci handbag on the cushioned chair next to the door. "I don't know how Gregory did it," she complained. "Taking care of everything at home by myself is so exhausting."

The nurse rolled her eyes. "Yeah, tell me about it."

Hilary ignored the sarcasm as she looked at Gregory. *Still in a coma? When is this going to be over, Gregory? You've got responsibilities at home and at your company. Your father won't get off my back about you getting back to work so he can get back to retirement and doesn't have to deal with William's inadequacies.*

She noticed that the reclining chair next to Gregory's bed, the luxury chair she'd ordered Eric to have brought into the room for her to sit on while she visited with Gregory, had been pushed away from the bed and sat against the wall. "That chair should be next to the bed," she snapped. "I can't sit next to Gregory when the chair is that far away."

The nurse briefly eyed the chair. "Well, don't that beat all." She went back to her business of fussing with Gregory's IV equipment.

Hilary took a deep breath and marched toward the drape-covered window, closed for privacy while the nurse was working in the room. *This nurse drives me crazy. I'll have to have a little talk with Eric about her.*

Parting the heavy drapes slightly with her newly manicured hands, she looked out over the property. Whispering Pines, an upscale private nursing facility, sat on ten acres of land within the boundaries of White Plains. The lawns were beautifully manicured, the bushes and trees precisely trimmed, some in the shape of animals.

Food could be purchased to feed the fish and ducks that lived in the large pond which sat in the middle of the property. Because of the high quality of the care, their services were only available to those who could afford to pay outrageous sums of money every day. For a hefty fee, Whispering Pines offered private rooms and the best nursing care money could buy. Hilary's social standing in the community required nothing less than the best for her husband. Still, she resented having to put so much money into something she couldn't spend on her own interests.

She turned away from the window. Alarmed that the nurse was removing the dressing from Gregory's arm, Hilary barked, "What are you doing?"

"Gettin' ready to take the IV out of his arm."

"Why?"

"It's my job." The nurse grinned unkindly and added, "Relax. It's time to switch it to the right arm. We switch it every three days. The left arm needs a break."

*It would be nice if they'd tell me these things*

*beforehand,* Hilary thought. "Is that normal?"

"Oh, sure, sweetie. Haven't you seen us do it before?"

Not wanting to seem like an idiot who didn't pay attention to little things, she manufactured an excuse. "Well, most of the time that type of thing is finished by the time I get here. And I've just been so concerned about Gregory's coma, I haven't paid that much attention to what the nurses are doing."

The nurse gave her an unsympathetic sideways glance that indicated she didn't buy the excuse.

Deciding it wasn't worth spending any more time discussing, Hilary put it out of her mind. With any luck, the nurse would finish quickly so Hilary could get on with her visit. She wanted to be alone when she spoke to Gregory.

Hilary folded her arms over her chest and studied the whiteboard hanging on the wall. It held Gregory's stats, medications, and nursing information. *Nothing new there*, she thought. She glanced at the oak nightstand that sat on one side of the bed. It held a phone and the remote for the flat-screen TV, hanging on the wall opposite Gregory's bed. *They charge me for all these amenities and Gregory can't appreciate any of it. What a waste.*

The room had been arranged to look like a comfortable bedroom with a chest of drawers to hold the medical equipment, sheets, and hospital gowns. Everything was always polished and in order.

Most of the technical equipment that had been in the room to monitor Gregory's vitals had been removed since his heart rate was always steady and he was able to breathe on his own.

Growing impatient with the nurse's unhurried stance, Hilary walked to the window again and parted the drapes. She had insisted he be on the ground floor so that she could have quicker access to him when she came to visit.

From the window, she looked across the manicured hedges to see a family with two young children, a boy and a girl, sitting on the grass next to the pond and eating a picnic lunch. An old, gray-haired woman sat forlornly in a wheelchair nearby. She wore a loose cashmere bathrobe over a hospital gown. The orderly caring for the woman laughed at something one of the children said. The old woman scowled.

On the sidewalk, closer to the building, a nurse pushed a wheelchair with a young boy of eight or nine. He had no hair. The boy watched the family eating and laughing, wishful thoughts showing clearly on his young face. An IV hung from a post fastened to the wheelchair. *Most likely cancer*, Hilary thought detachedly.

She turned around, catching a glimpse of herself in a mirror hanging on one wall. The bright lighting in the room made the highlights of her newly styled brunette hair look dull. She made a mental note to tell her beautician about the problem at her next appointment. The lighting also made her face look thinner and older than normal. She grimaced at the thought that she was in her mid-forties and the next decade would be hitting too soon. With a freshly manicured hand, she smoothed out her custom-tailored Gucci floral-embroidered jacket. *Thank goodness, the matching slacks look as fresh as they had this morning when I'd put them on. And that's why I only buy the best,* she thought, raising her chin.

Hilary looked down at her $4000 watch, then glanced at the nurse again. "How long are you going to be?" she demanded.

"Before I remove the IV from Greg's left arm," the nurse said in a slow, condescending tone, "I want to prepare a new one for his right arm. Then, I will be able to switch the lines without losin' a lot of time in between. I need to get everything ready first. Then I will start."

Hilary huffed, "His name is Gregory, not Greg, and I

didn't ask for a play-by-play. I asked how long you would be."

The nurse turned her head to face Hilary squarely. "As long as it takes, ma'am. Sometimes it goes fast. Sometimes it goes slow. Depends on how cooperative the patient is."

Hilary smirked. "How uncooperative can he be? He's been in a coma for a week. Just stick it in him and get on with it so I can have my visit. I'm tired. I want to go home."

The nurse placed a protective hand on Gregory's arm. "Just stick 'em, huh? Sorry, but it don't work that way. I'm gonna take my time and do my job right. You don't like that, take it up with my supervisor." She turned her back to continue her work, her wide hips blocking Hilary's view.

Hilary prickled. She narrowed her eyes. This turn of events forced her into an uncomfortable position, even though she knew she was wrong about rushing the nurse in this situation. The hired help had no right to talk down to her like that. *This nurse is pushing all the wrong buttons. She's about to find out just what kind of influence I have. I don't pay a fortune to this place every day to be treated this way.* "We'll just see about that," Hilary hissed over her shoulder as she snatched up her purse and stormed out of the room.

\* \* \*

Hilary barged into the luxurious corner office that belonged to Eric Bolanger, Executive Director of Whispering Pines. A short pudgy man, he immediately stood up.

His secretary, Mona, followed closely behind Hilary. "Sorry, Mr. Bolanger. I tried to stop her but—"

"It's okay, Mona. I'll take care of it." Eric straightened his expensive suit jacket and tie as he moved out from behind his antique mahogany desk.

Mona turned and left, her shoes making little to no noise on the strategically placed runners that protected the cushy, beige carpet that covered the floor. She closed the door quietly behind her.

Hilary, already in a bad mood from dealing with the nurse in Gregory's room, was further infuriated when Mona left without the courtesy of acknowledging her. *What a witch.* And Hilary hated the cheerful, happy pictures of Eric with well-known and easily recognized clients that hung on the wall adjacent to the door. Diplomas and awards vied for space on the wall behind the desk. Sunlight poured in through the wall-to-wall windows on the other two walls.

"And what has my staff done this time?" Eric asked, a shadow of worry flashing across his middle-aged chubby face. He briefly glanced at his thick Rolex watch.

"Gregory's nurse moved my chair. It was clear over against the wall," Hilary growled. "And she is taking her sweet time changing his IV. She's cutting into my visiting time. Can't she do these things before I get here so I don't have to wait to visit my husband?"

Eric sighed. "Hilary, I applaud your faithfulness to your husband, but—"

"Don't *but* me," Hilary snapped. Her spiked heels sunk into the carpet as she came face to face with him. "I don't want excuses. I want uninterrupted visits. I'm paying you a fortune every day he's here, and I think I deserve to be accommodated."

"I realize that," Eric explained, backing off a little, "but we need to take care of Gregory's needs on *our* schedule, mainly because it's impossible to know when you will show up."

Hilary's eyes widened. "Now I'm supposed to make

an appointment?" She glared at him, her lips pursed tightly, her body defiant. "I don't think so."

"No, no, nothing like that," Eric apologized, putting up his hands in a conciliatory gesture. "You can come when you want."

"And the chair?" She was not going to back down. This kind of stuff had been going on long enough, and it seemed to be getting worse. She was going to get more accommodation.

"As for the chair, the nurses need to be able to get to Gregory to take care of him. If the chair gets in the way, they will move it, but they will always move it back where it belongs. I'll see to it."

"Well, talk to your help. I don't want any more disruptions than necessary in Gregory's recovery."

Eric sighed and moved behind his desk. He sat down, picked up a pen, and toyed with it. He looked Hilary in the eye and his tone of voice became more authoritative. "I've told you, Hilary, just because Gregory showed a small physical response five days ago, doesn't mean he's coming out of his coma. When you were rubbing his hand, it could have been just a random muscle spasm causing his hand to seem like he was shaking you off."

"He was trying to tell me something. He wants me to know he knows I'm here."

"The neurologist and other specialists have made it clear to you that he's had a brain injury and there's no guarantee that he will come out of it any time soon. Comas are unpredictable. It's true that many people come out of a coma within four weeks, but there is often significant damage. Some have a long road to physical recovery. Some never recover mentally.

"From the doctor's tests, there are no signs of any new brain activity in Gregory, nor a response to any external stimuli. I don't see how the movement of his hand on one day proves anything. It was just a muscle spasm.. It could be weeks, months, years or maybe nev—"

"Don't say it," Hilary snapped. "I refuse to believe he won't recover. Look at him. He looks like a normal healthy person, sleeping peacefully. You can't tell me he'll just lay there like a vegetable for the rest of his life. You agreed with me the other day that his moving hand might be a good sign."

He spluttered, "Well, yes, I did, but I spoke too soon. We haven't seen any other signs since. I also told you not to get your hopes up."

"That's not acceptable."

"And as for my staff," he said, changing the subject, "they're doing the best job they can under the circumstances."

She glared at him a long moment. *Okay, then, you need to see what I have to deal with on my visits.* She started toward the door and turned to him. "Now, if you'll be so kind as to come with me."

Eric dropped the pen on the desk. A look of shock registered on his face. "Why?"

"To talk to the nurse, of course. I'm tired and I want to go home, but first I need to spend some time with my husband. I can't do that with a nurse banging around the room." She walked out the door, not waiting to see if he would follow or not, but expecting him to obey, as he always did.

By the time she passed two doors down the hall, she heard Eric's shoes slapping on the highly polished wooden floor. He rushed to meet up with her.

*Ha, I knew he'd follow me. He can be so spineless.*

They walked together in silence to Gregory's room.

\* \* \*

As they entered the room, Hilary noticed the

obnoxious heavyset nurse still bent over Gregory. She was getting ready to insert the new IV into his right arm.

Perturbed with the nurse, Hilary walked to the bedside and took Gregory's left hand.

Suddenly, Gregory seemed to be jerking his arm away from the nurse, as if she was hurting him.

Hilary squeezed Gregory's hand. "See, Eric," she exclaimed, "he is coming out of the coma. He's aware enough to know he doesn't need the IV tube anymore."

The nurse shot her a glower, knowing the dig was meant for her. She continued to struggle to get the needle into his arm.

"What's going on, nurse?" Eric asked, drawing closer to the bed. He stopped, however, far enough from the patient that, should there be an *accident* and blood shoot out of Gregory's body, he wouldn't get anything on his prim clothing or catch some germs. At least, that's the impression Hilary always got when Eric came into Gregory's room. As far as she knew, he was only a figurehead and left the care of the patients to the specialists on his staff.

The nurse managed to finish putting the IV into Gregory's arm and he immediately settled down. "Don't know why he was fighting me, Mr. Bolanger," the nurse said. "I couldn't seem to get the needle in right."

"Did you see that?" Hilary shouted as she squeezed Gregory's hand again.

"What?" Eric said, coming a little closer to the bed.

"I thought I saw his eyes flicker for a moment."

The nurse checked under Gregory's eyelids to see if he was awake. "Seems to be quiet. Same as he was before."

"He's coming out of the coma," Hilary insisted with a growing feeling of hope and excitement. "It's a sign."

"It's not that simple, Hilary. It could be a sign, but maybe not. We've seen these kinds of temporary muscle spasms in many coma patients. Random responses can be deceiving." He spoke to the nurse. "Has he been showing other signs of increased stimuli like this?"

"No," the nurse said begrudgingly, frowning at Hilary as if she wished Gregory would come out of his damn coma and leave the premises so she wouldn't have to deal with Hilary any more.

Hilary refused to have her hopes dampened. "His eyes flickered. He moved his arm. This is good news, Eric."

Eric hesitated in his wishy-washy way. "Again, we don't want to get our hopes up too much. We still have no idea if he will come out of it."

Once more, Hilary squeezed Gregory's hand in hers. Her budding hope turned to slight disappointment when he didn't squeeze back or respond in any other way. Despite that, a million heartening thoughts flashed through her mind at this latest development. Foremost, that Gregory would come around and be able to go back to work in his company, and that her home and social life would return to normal.

"Monday morning," Eric said, "I'll have the doctor making the rounds bring in some monitors and do some tests. We'll see how Gregory reacts to various kinds of stimuli."

"Do it now," Hilary demanded.

"The doctor isn't here and he won't do tests like that over the weekend, unless it's an emergency. We'll just have to wait."

Hilary bristled in silence. "But if he wakes up tonight, I want a phone call. I don't care how late it is." She moved toward the door. "I'll talk to you in the morning."

"Are you leaving so soon?" the nurse blurted. "What about your precious visit?"

Eric glared at the nurse.

"Yes, I'm leaving. I've had all I can take today. You ruined my visit, but at least I have the satisfaction of knowing my visits here may be coming to an end. Once Gregory comes out of this coma, we can move him to our house and hire a *decent* private nurse until he's completely well."

Not missing the dig at one of his employees, Eric shook his head and sighed. "Come on, Hilary, I'll walk you to the door."

"Good," she asserted, standing in the doorway. "On the way, we can discuss how you're going to change Gregory's nursing schedule. I don't want this nurse around him anymore."

"I'm just doing my job," the nurse shot back.

Hilary ignored her and motioned for Eric to follow her as she walked out of the room. Continuing down the hall, she said, "She may not have done anything wrong, but she's full of negative energy. I don't want her around Gregory anymore. Do I make myself clear?"

"Crystal clear," Eric muttered.

Hilary rolled her eyes. *God, I can't wait until Gregory gets well. I'm so tired of dealing with these people. I just want my life back the way it was.*

# Chapter 3

## Lake Havasu City, AZ

Five days had passed since that night on the couch when I'd had the funny feeling in my hand. I hadn't thought much about it. Today, I was on a job replacing a couple of cracked floor tiles in a kitchen. Country music drifted in from the TV in the front room.

Three Shih Tzu dogs watched me intently from their travel cages set against the far wall. From the evil looks the dogs gave me, and occasionally a low growl, I wasn't sure if they were watching to make sure I did the job right, or to make sure I wasn't a crazy killer there to attack, rape, and murder their mom, Mary, a tall, thin elegant lady who stood at the sink washing her morning dishes. Bent over on my knees on the floor, I scraped up the old thin-set and tried to ignore the dogs.

Suddenly, a sharp pain stabbed me in the elbow pit of my right arm, like someone sticking me with a needle. Grabbing it with my left hand, I winced and sat back.

"What's the matter?" Mary asked, looking down at me with concern, her short, loose grey hair flopping against her face.

"Nothing's wrong," I lied, holding my arm. The feeling wasn't going away. I stood up and rubbed my arm as I held it close to my body. "I'm okay."

"It doesn't look like nothing," she said, coming closer.

"Are you sure you're alright?" She frowned, growing more serious. "You aren't having a heart attack, are you?"

I wasn't sure, but I didn't want to worry her. "I think it's a pinched nerve or maybe I pulled a small muscle." I could still feel a needle-like stabbing pain. I'd given blood on occasion and had blood drawn for tests. This felt similar, but a lot more painful and longer-lasting. "I'm fine," I said, easing up on my arm to reassure her it wasn't a problem. "Maybe it's just a cramp."

Her eyes moved from my face to my arm and back to my face. She shrugged. "Okay, if you say so. I've got some things to do in the back room. Call me if you need me for anything." She put down the dish towel and left the room.

The pain suddenly disappeared, but now it felt as though someone was messing with my arm, taping down a bandage or something. Shivers shot up and down my spine. "Okay," I mumbled to myself, "this is really starting to freak me out."

I pinched my offending skin with the thumb and fingers of my left hand and squeezed hard. I rubbed it vigorously. I slapped it. Nothing seemed to work.

Finally, the feeling instantly stopped. Like it had never happened.

"This is just too weird." Bending and straightening my elbow a few times, I wanted to make sure I couldn't feel anything strange. When nothing further happened, I shook my head and went back to my knees to finish my work.

I found myself constantly on edge that I might get another attack. Thankfully, the rest of the day passed with nothing else out of the ordinary.

That night, when I called Chrissy, I almost told her about the new feeling. At the last second, I changed my mind. I wasn't sure what was going on with me and I didn't want her to worry or to make her think I was making all this up. Besides, I was doing enough worrying for the both of us.

# Chapter 4

"**W**ell?" Hilary asked Eric as Mona led her into his office late Monday morning. "Did the doctor do the tests this morning?"

Eric grabbed a manila envelope on his desk and opened it. "Yes, he did. And the results weren't all that encouraging."

"What do you mean?" Hilary demanded, staring down at him.

He motioned toward a chair. "Would you like to sit down?"

"No, I wouldn't. What were the results?"

"I'm sorry, Hilary, but Gregory didn't respond to any of the stimuli tests the doctor gave him. His brain activity didn't change at all on the monitor."

"Then, how do you explain his reaction to the nurse changing his IV on Friday? We saw his arm move and I saw his eyes flicker. And last week, when Gregory flinched as I was rubbing the back of his hand. What about that? Did you tell the doctor?"

"Yes, I told him. Random muscle spasms, he says. It's not that unusual for coma patients. Sometimes they even open their eyes and make sounds, but then they fall asleep again for weeks or months."

Hilary stamped her foot. "No. I don't want to hear

this. I won't accept this." She couldn't bear the thought that Gregory wouldn't be around to make her life normal again. He looked perfectly normal. Why was he doing this to her?

Eric opened his mouth to say something more, but she cut him off.

"You can believe what you want, but I have to believe he's getting better. He's going to come out of this thing, whatever it is, and I'll be there to see it. Until that time, I suggest you keep an open mind, and maybe you should get another doctor's opinion." She turned on her heels and headed for the door.

"I'll be in Gregory's room," she said without looking back, "and I don't want to be interrupted by the nurses today."

\* \* \*

Hilary sat on the edge of her plush recliner and reached out to touch Gregory's hand. The soft hum of music from the hallway played quietly in the background. She gave Gregory's hand a few hard pushes, but she got no response.

"You've got to come out of this, Gregory. You have to. Don't listen to the doctors and the nurses. They don't know you like I do. You always make things work right. You always get things done. You've built successful businesses and made us a lot of money. You can come out of this. I know you've been responding because you're trying to tell me something. You're trying to reach out to me."

The frustration she had been holding back suddenly overwhelmed her again. "But I wish you'd hurry. I'm so tired of handling everything by myself. I don't like having to deal with Nick, our maintenance man. He seems to be getting lazier every day. The children are getting on my nerves. Your father is always on my back about you getting back to the company. And not only all that, people are starting to talk. They are wondering what will happen to the company if you don't get better. Even worse, they are asking me what I will do if you don't get better." *Who will take care of me? What will happen to my social standing?* She couldn't bear to think about that outcome.

She stood up and paced back and forth on the polished floor. "Brittney and Jonathan are driving me crazy. I've been in a couple of hard arguments with them in the last few days. Without you there to mediate, nothing is getting resolved."

The drapes had been pulled back from the window, streaming light into the room. She walked to the window and peered out over the lawns. "Brittney insists that she's not ready to go to college yet. She says she needs another year or two to *find herself*. She's thinking of taking another trip to Europe."

Hilary laughed. "She's such a loser. I told her she was twenty-five-years-old and, if she hadn't found herself by now, she'd better hurry or life was going to pass her by. She'll end up an old lonely woman wondering what happened. All of her friends, the ones who decided to go to college, have already graduated. If she doesn't hurry, she'll be the oldest one in her classes. I don't think she'd tolerate going to school with a bunch of young kids. Personally, I think she's too old for college. She needs to find a rich guy, get married, and start having children of her own.

"Then she could start volunteering her time to the community. Which would give her a decent standing socially, instead of hanging out with gender-challenged new-agers who are going nowhere in life."

The scene outside the window looked the same as the

day before. Just different faces. *Same shit, different day,* she thought. Turning from the window, she leaned back against the sill. "At least one of our three children is mature enough to help me handle a few things until you get better. It's amazing how our youngest and our oldest ended up being so . . . how should I put it, immature? Thank God for William. Problem is, he's spending almost all of his time trying to keep your company going, so his time has been limited to help me."

She walked back to the bed. Starting to feel antsy, she stared down at her husband. "Come back, Gregory," she pleaded. "I don't know how long I can keep this up without you. I have social commitments and engagements that I'm missing because of you being here. I need you. Your father and William are handling the company, but your father is getting frustrated and difficult. He says he's retired and he doesn't want to work. William can't handle the company by himself. He hasn't had enough experience.

"Even with the two of them working together, we are losing money. William says they are on the verge of losing a startup business you'd been working on. He estimates we could lose three million if it falls through. You are the only one who can handle those kinds of complicated transactions."

She poked him in the chest a couple of times. "Don't force me to do something drastic. You are wasting time and money lying here. Come out of this coma thing, Gregory. *Now!*"

No response.

She sighed, turned toward the door, and picked up her purse. "I have to get some lunch."

\* \* \*

In the afternoon, Hilary found herself seated again in the recliner in Gregory's room. She closed her tired eyes and wallowed in a bad mood. She wracked her brain about what to do to get Gregory to wake up.

*Maybe I'm not giving Gregory enough physical attention, something to draw him out of his coma, something to make him want to wake up and come home. Rubbing his hand was one thing, but he could possibly need more. Maybe I need to have more direct contact with him. At least, it might be worth a try.*

She pulled herself out of the chair and sat on the edge of the bed near the headboard. "I think I can do better than I've been doing," she said to him, trying to sound affectionate. "I'll get closer to you."

She clumsily slid one arm under his shoulder to bring his head to rest against her chest. With her free hand, she ran her fingers through his light brown hair from the brow to the top of his head. It felt strange being physical with him. They had had three children, but even though they slept in the same bed, they hadn't had sex in years. Holding hands, kissing, and all other forms of affectionate displays had never held much of a stronghold in their relationship. She felt awkward and inexperienced as her hand brushed his hair and her fingers ran down the sides of his temples.

Suddenly, Gregory jerked his head back and forth in weak, irregular motions.

Hilary's heart leaped in shock. *Oh, my god. Is he waking up?* She held on and stroked his head again, hoping that his eyes would open.

His arms seemed to want to move, making small lifting motions. His head became more vigorous, tossing from side to side. His hands shifted as he continued to try to lift his arms without avail.

She pulled her arm from under his shoulders and

jumped up. A thrill ran up her spine. "Did my rubbing your head wake you up? Are you trying to communicate with me? Oh, my god, the doctor needs to see this. Eric needs to see this."

Hilary hurried around the side of the bed and pressed the call button. Waiting anxiously for the nurse to respond, she stood over the bed and put her hand on Gregory's shifting arm. She watched him seem to still struggle slightly in his sleep. Her excitement continued to grow.

"Someone has to see this," she said, unable to sit still any longer. "Someone has to see you responding to my stimulus." She got up and looked at her watch. She feared that if she left the room to find a nurse or Eric, Gregory would quiet down and no one would believe her.

Peeking out the door, she saw only an empty hallway. *Where the hell are they?* She returned to the bed and pushed the call button again and again. She grabbed her cellphone out of her purse and tried calling Eric. No answer from his secretary or office. *Damn.*

At that moment, Gregory's arms fell limply to his side. His head stopped moving.

"You can't do this to me," Hilary said, shaking his arm and shoulder a few times. "Gregory, wake up. Wake up!" Desperate to get him into action again, she sat near the headboard and rubbed his forehead. She stroked his hair, making sure he felt her fingernails scrape against his skin. Nothing.

Five minutes later, a nurse finally arrived. "Is something wrong?"

Hilary stood angrily by the side of the bed. "As long as it took you to get here, my husband could have been dead if something had been wrong."

"I'm sorry," the nurse said, moving closer to the bed and picking up Gregory's wrist to check his pulse. "I was busy in an emergency with another patient."

Hilary placed her hands on her hips. "And I suppose you are the only nurse working today?"

"No, Miss, but—"

"Never mind." Hilary marched out of the room. *It's time I have another talk with Eric.*

# Chapter 5

Lake Havasu City, AZ

It was three days before I experienced the third *episode*. That's what I was calling them now: *episodes*. I was documenting them, too. I noted when they happened, what I was doing at the time, and where I was located. I also kept track of everything I ate and drank, thinking that, if this was an allergy of some type, I could isolate it on my own. I wasn't about to go to a doctor about this. Not yet anyway.

This third time, my hair was affected. Well, my head, too. I kept my hair cut pretty short, maybe a half-inch at the longest. I didn't wear hats.

I had been leaning forward, replacing the cover on an electrical outlet on a kitchen backsplash, when it suddenly felt like someone was running a hand through the hair on the top of my head. I turned around, expecting to see the homeowner with a grin on his face, but there was no one there.

The feeling grew more intense, moving from my forehead to the top of my head, then to the sides. It sort of tickled, like fingers running through my hair. With my hands, I rubbed vigorously at my head. The feeling didn't stop, and in fact, my scalp started to itch. I scratched at it until I feared I would draw blood. Still, the funny feeling of someone running their fingers over my head persisted.

Desperately, I stuck my head under the faucet at the sink. At this point, I stopped caring what the homeowner or anyone else might think if they came into the room. Turning on the cold water, I soaked my hair, letting the wetness flow across my tortured scalp. It seemed to help. I stayed there for a few minutes when, suddenly, the funny feelings faded away.

I shut off the faucet and used my hands to squeegee the water off my head. I grabbed a dish towel that was hanging on the handle of the stove door and dabbed at my hair. I looked to make sure I hadn't drawn blood. No blood. Goosebumps ran up and down my arms. I was growing more and more freaked out.

Thankfully, I did manage to finish the job without electrocuting myself.

On the way home, I called Chrissy. I didn't want to tell her about the episodes, and I didn't want her to see me in a worried mood.

"Hi, sweetie," she chirped in greeting.

"Hi," I said, trying to sound lighthearted. "I'm afraid I might be coming down with something, so maybe you shouldn't come over tonight." I felt bad lying to her, but I didn't know what other excuse she would accept.

"Are you sure? I could bring you some soup or something?"

"No, really, I'm fine. I just want to go home and lay down. I'm really tired. I'll call you tomorrow, okay?"

"Okay," she agreed. "But call me if you need anything and I'll come right over."

"Thanks, but I think I'll be fine." I hung up before she could say anything more.

At home, I took a long shower and hoped it would relax me. It didn't do the job. I ate dinner and watched the evening news, thinking maybe the problems of the world would take my mind off my little problem. That didn't help.

Was I losing my mind? The thought passed before me several times. I didn't think I could be losing my mind, but then, again, I'd never gone crazy in the past. Only time would tell if this was the beginning of a slow spiral into insanity, or if it was going to be a passing thing.

Puttering around the house, I cleaned a little, dusted the coffee table and TV. I tried reading a book, but I couldn't concentrate. *Maybe I should have let Chrissy come over. At least, I'd have someone to talk to.* I considered taking Sadie for a walk, but she was sleeping soundly in her bed, and I hated to wake her up. Plus, I didn't feel like going outside.

Inspired, I picked up my phone and dialed my daughter, Megan, who lived in Golden, Colorado. She had stayed with my parents there while she went to college in Denver. She liked the area so much, when she graduated a year ago, she moved into her own apartment in Golden. Says she liked Denver okay, but I say she stays in Golden because my parents spoil her. It's good for all of them, especially since I live so far from my mom and dad and don't get that much chance to see them.

We talked for a half-hour. I was careful not to mention anything about my little episodes. The last thing I needed was for Megan to tell my mom, who worried about everything. When I was young and first moved away from home, it took me a long time to convince my mom we didn't need to talk every day. The first time we went a week without talking I figured she would go crazy, but she said it wasn't that bad. It got better over time. Now, years later, we can go two or three months without talking and she's fine with it.

After hanging up with Megan, I called my parents. That took care of my obligatory phone call for the next month. By the time I got off the phone, I noticed over an hour had passed.

Just to pass more time, I thought about calling my sister in Denver. We had drifted apart over the years and didn't seem to get along very well. She didn't like the fact that I lived so far away and didn't visit our parents very often. She felt burdened that I had left her to care for our parents alone as they were aging. I didn't believe they were that needy and were doing perfectly fine on their own, both being in good health.

The last time I'd been in Denver, she and I had gotten into quite an argument about all that. In the end, we agreed to disagree and went our separate ways with bad feelings on both sides. I didn't like it, but she was so stubborn, it was hard to deal with her. So, I didn't call her.

I let Sadie out the back door to do her thing, then I gave her a bedtime snack. She snarfed it up and sacked out as I got ready for bed. Sadie was getting up there in years and seemed to want to sleep most of the time.

I went to bed, but I found I couldn't sleep. I was dreading my next episode. I couldn't help but wonder which part of my body might be affected next. As I lay there, staring at the dark ceiling, I found that I was starting to have a sort of morbid fascination with my body. I found myself checking in with all my different parts—arms, legs, hands, feet, head—gauging to see if any of them were having any kind of funny feelings.

Finally, I drifted off to sleep. In a dream, I saw a car coming head-on toward me at full-speed. I woke up screaming.

# Chapter 6

White Plains, NY

Hilary had convinced Eric to have the doctor do another set of tests that same week. This time, she insisted on being in the room when they were performed. She didn't like having to get to the nursing facility early in the morning when the doctor made his rounds, but she compromised and managed to make it to Gregory's room before the doctor had finished.

As usual, Eric stood a little distance from the bed. Hilary stood next to him and watched the elderly doctor lift the sheet off Gregory's feet, exposing Gregory's soles and toes.

"This is the last test," the doctor said to Hilary over his spectacles. He seemed perturbed, like she had wasted his time redoing these tests the second time this week. "So far, we've had no response from any of the tests this morning, including pricking and pinching his skin."

"Isn't there more you can do than that?" Hilary asked.

"Short of flaying him," the nurse mumbled.

"I heard that," Hilary barked. She glared at the overweight nurse she'd been trying to get banned for the last few days. Unfortunately, Eric had all kinds of excuses for keeping her there. She was still being a pain in the neck.

The doctor pulled a pen out of the pocket of his white

smock. He grabbed Gregory's right foot by the toes and held them firmly. He pressed the cap side of the pen against Gregory's heel and pushed hard. He then pushed the pen into the center of the foot, hard enough to leave an indent. No reaction. The doctor ran the pen across Gregory's toes several times without a response.

Shaking his head, as though to say this is exactly what he had expected, the doctor put the pen in his pocket and covered Gregory's feet with the sheet. "I'm sorry, Mrs. Nordmeyer, even though your husband occasionally *seems* to be reacting to certain stimulus, there has not been enough activity to indicate that he'll be coming out of this state any time soon. Little movements are *not* conclusive evidence, by any means." He picked up his bag to leave.

"That's it?" Hilary shrieked, outraged that no one would believe her. "All you do is run a pen down his foot and because there is no response, you say there is no change? What about his reaction to me the other day? You can't say that was just a muscle spasm."

The doctor stared at her hard. "Mrs. Nordmeyer, you can't force things that have their own timing. I will not promise you that your husband is coming out of this state. You can make of it what you want, but we are doing everything we can to keep him comfortable and alive with proper treatments, physical therapy, and nursing care. Now, I have other patients to see. I'm already behind my schedule." He left without giving her time to answer.

Hilary turned to Eric, who seemed to be cowering nervously, anticipating her onslaught. "In this building, in any hospital, there's not one machine . . . not one damn modern medical marvel that can properly diagnose my husband's case? Great, just great."

"We've had other tests done, Hilary," Eric said defensively. "You know that. We've done all the standard tests and more. We've put him on machines that can read his physical functions and track his brain waves. The results are nil. Modern medicine hasn't advanced enough to go beyond reading electronic signals when a brain isn't functioning right."

"Well, I'm not satisfied. This isn't what I bargained for when I brought Gregory here. I expected more help."

Eric's shoulders dropped. Even in his well-fitted suit, which hid the pouch of his overweight body, he looked defeated.

This, too, infuriated Hilary. *Such a loser.*

A knock at the door caught Hilary's attention. An orderly stuck his head inside and said, "Mr. Bolanger, the doctor would like to see you for a moment."

After he left, Hilary glared at the nurse, who checked the IV bag then quickly left the room.

Standing over the bed, Hilary could hardly contain her anger. *Gregory, why are you doing this to me? Why are you making a fool out of me?* She went to her purse and took out a pen. She walked to the end of the bed and lifted his covers. "Tell me you aren't going to respond to this." She jabbed the cap end of the pen against his foot and held it there.

Gregory's leg jerked as if he was trying to move his foot away from the pain.

"Ah ha, you *are* waking up. You know I'm here, don't you?" She jabbed the pen into a couple of other places, then ran the pen up and down his foot. She went to the head of the bed and roughly lifted one of his eyelids to see if he was awake. She nearly poked him in the eye.

His head rolled to the side to move away from her.

"They can't tell me you aren't waking up and that your foot and your eye reactions just now were little muscle spasms." She pressed the call button then went to the door to find Eric. He was already heading for Gregory's room with the overweight nurse in tow.

Hilary resented the staff even more for never getting to the room on time to see Gregory's movements. "By the way, Eric," she said belligerently as he came into the room, "your nurse's response time sucks. It could use a lot of improvement."

Eric held his hand up, cutting off a reply from the nurse. "The nurse is here now. She responded immediately to your call. If you are referring to Gregory's response to you rubbing his head the other day, there is still no evidence it was more than random muscle movements or contractions or—"

"No!" Hilary shouted. "That's what you've been saying every time Gregory reacts to me. I know differently. Just now, he responded again. Why won't you believe me?"

Eric looked at Gregory's silent body lying on the bed. "What did he do?"

"He moved his foot and his head when I touched them."

Eric grimaced, not knowing what to say. He looked at the nurse, then back to Hilary.

"I'm telling you, he moved again," she insisted, "and it wasn't a little muscle spasm."

Eric remained at a loss for words. After a few moments, his manner softened and his voice lowered. He seemed a little hesitant as he changed the subject. "The doctor wanted me to discuss something with you. What about having other members of your family visit? What about your children? Maybe it would be good for Gregory to have some contact with them. Maybe they would help him come around."

Caught off-guard, Hilary felt uncomfortable with this new line of questioning. All the steam in her anger started to fizzle. She didn't want to admit to Eric that there were a lot of relationship problems in the family.

Eric went on. "There's a new therapy that is being

tried on coma patients. Members of the family come in for a number of hours each day and use visual, auditory, and physical stimulus that might stir the patient's memory and awaken him. The doctor said there has been significant improvements in a some patients after the implementation of that therapy."

Careful not to commit to anything, she said, "Well, I'll see what I can do." She already knew that Brittney and Jonathan refused to visit any hospitals or care facilities. They said sick people repulsed them. And William was way too busy with the company business to drop by during the day. He kept promising to visit, but hadn't made it in all week.

Eric spoke again. "Didn't you mentioned his mother and father live close by? Maybe they could come visit? The presence of his parents might help jar him out of this state."

"Like I said, I'll see what I can do." She turned toward Gregory's bed. "Now, if you don't mind, I'd like to spend some quality time with my husband."

Looking relieved, Eric motioned the nurse out the door. Under his breath, Hilary heard him say, "Take your time, Hilary. It'll keep you out of my hair for a while." He pulled the door shut behind him.

Hilary sat on the recliner. The thought of asking Gregory's parents to visit disturbed her. They had never been there for him. More or less, he had been raised by nannies and put in boarding schools. As an only child, Gregory had seemed to get in the way of his parents. With their jet-setting lifestyle, social obligations, and business dealings, they were too busy to be bothered by the demands of a child, even if that child was their own flesh and blood. But that didn't stop them from expecting Gregory to take over the family business when he came of age.

When Gregory graduated from college, he refused to

obey the command of his parents to learn how to run their company. Instead, he went on to build his own fortune in his own way. After some years of gaining experience in the business world, and knowing that his father wanted to retire soon, he took over his father's company and built it into a solid financial empire. Ironically, Gregory turned out to be a far better businessman than his father.

She looked at Gregory, lying quietly and unmoving under the sheets. No, she didn't expect his parents to visit. And neither would he. He didn't love them. He only tolerated them for the sake of social expectations.

She didn't feel like talking to Gregory today. Things were not going as she wished and she didn't have anything to say. It made her angry that he was getting off so easily by lying in a coma while she struggled with all the hassles caused by his absence at home and at the company. She left the room quietly and hoped no one would notice and judge her for leaving so early.

# Chapter 7

## Lake Havasu City, AZ

It happened again four days later on a Thursday morning. I was tearing out an old deck so I could replace it with a new one. Mid-September in Lake Havasu could still get pretty hot. If I was working outside, like I was today, I made sure to be on the job by five in the morning.

On these kinds of jobs, I'd tried taking Sadie to work with me right after I got her. But she didn't like the machine noises I had to make while I was working. Actually, I think she preferred lying around the house sleeping all day while I was gone. How boring. What a life she had. Eat, sleep, and poop. Repeat. Boring!

By nine o'clock, I had all the boards pulled off and was gathering them up to throw in my pickup. Boards were scattered everywhere, along with screws and a few nails.

Walking toward my truck, I held an armful of boards when I felt pain in my right foot. I thought I had stepped on a nail or a screw. Since I was only a few feet from my truck, I hopped on one foot until I could manage to throw the boards over the side of the bed. Strangely, the pain grew more intense. I sat on the tailgate, quickly unlaced my work boot, and pulled the boot and sweaty sock off as fast as I could. I could see nothing wrong, no marks, no blood.

A shiver ran up my spine. It was another episode. The pain moved from the middle of my foot, to my heel, and then to the ball of my foot.

Faintly, I heard someone say, "You know I'm here." But when I glanced around, no one could be seen. *Must have been a TV or radio or something.*

As I sat there rubbing my foot, it felt like someone was running a pointed object slowly up and down the sole of my foot. In a way, it tickled. No matter what I did, I couldn't get it to stop. I wondered if I had something wrong with one of the nerves in my foot. Maybe it was getting pinched.

I was so involved trying to figure out what was going on, I didn't see the homeowner come from the house.

"Ya didn't hurt yerself did ya? 'Cause I won't let ya file a claim on my insurance. You'll have ta use yer own."

I gave him a reassuring smile. "No, I'm fine. It's just a cramp." *What the heck, it worked before with Mary. Why not use it again?* It was all I could do to keep from digging at my foot and screaming at the top of my lungs while he stood there.

He crossed his arms and glared at me. "Better be fine. Don't want no more problems from contractors." With that, he turned on his heel and sauntered away.

Now that he was gone, I could at least dig at my foot and curse under my breath.

As usual, the pain stopped. The abrupt starting and stopping of these funny feelings led me to believe it wasn't my imagination. This was something physical. Suddenly, a pain exploded in my right eye. It only lasted for a couple of seconds, then it was gone. I blinked to focus my eyes again.

I heard the faint voice again. It was too quiet to hear exactly what it was saying, but it sounded like, "They can't tell me . . . foot . . . eye . . . just now . . ."

I looked around me on all sides as chills ran down my back. The part about the foot and the eye hit too close to home. I was wondering if someone was playing a practical joke on me. But there was no one around. The other houses sat far enough away that a person would have to yell in order for me to hear them. This voice was quiet, as if a person was speaking right next me.

Ever since the second episode, I had kept track of everything I ate, and I hadn't eaten anything out of the ordinary, so I knew it wasn't a food allergy. I seriously doubted it could be caused by pollens in the air.

Truthfully, with each episode, I was getting more frightened. They seemed to be lasting longer and getting more intense. I wondered if the voices were associated with the episodes. I couldn't imagine what that might mean.

I put my sock and boot back on and finished the job. My senses stayed on high alert for any unusual feelings the rest of the day. None appeared.

*       *       *

That night, I blurted it all out to Chrissy while she ate her spaghetti.

"You're imagining them," she said as she flipped back her auburn hair and picked up a forkful of spaghetti.

Feeling lost, alone, and hurt, I almost started crying. I ducked my head to hide my quivering lip. "I'm not imagining them, Chrissy," I said slowly and quietly. "They're real. I don't know what's causing them, but I'm getting worried. I think maybe I'm going crazy or something."

She got out of her chair and walked around behind me. Wrapping her arms around my shoulders, she held me tight. "I'm sorry. I didn't realize you were so upset about them. I doubt if you're going crazy. You're the most grounded, stable person I think I've ever met. Could it be from too much stress at work? Maybe you need to take a few days off."

"I don't know I—"

"Hey, I know." She released me from her bear hug. "Slide your chair back."

Curious, I obeyed and slid my chair away from the table.

She threw her leg across my legs and straddled me, face to face, her hands locked behind my neck. "Why don't we go away for the weekend? Vegas, L.A., San Diego. It's your choice." Her blue eyes, looking bright and hopeful, searched mine.

Intuitively, I knew a few days away wouldn't make a difference. She had no idea how real, how intense the feelings had been. No matter where I went, I feared they would follow me and be the same. But, on the other hand, I knew she'd been working hard lately, too. Maybe she needed the break as much, or more, than I did. "Sure. I have to finish a job tomorrow, so let's leave early on Saturday morning."

She smiled widely. "Great. I can't wait. But you need to let me know where we're going so I know what clothes to take." She bounced in my lap. "So where are we going? You do know, don't you?"

I laughed. "It doesn't matter to me." Taking her face in my hands, I planted a kiss on her lips. "I have a funny feeling we'll never get out of the hotel room, no matter where we go."

She shoved away from me and stood up. "Don't bet on it, lover boy. I'm ready to dance up a storm and party all Saturday night."

I watched her walk back to her chair. Her hips swung in time to the tune she was humming.

I said, "You'll have to find somebody younger than me if you're planning on partying all night long."

"Not to worry." She smiled mischievously. "Rich Vegas playboy, L.A. movie star, or San Diego surfer, I'm sure I can find somebody to replace you if you can't keep up."

"I guess I'd better plan on a late night then, huh?"

"Don't worry, I won't run you too ragged. But I do want to take your mind off these episodes and help you have a little fun for a change."

Fun I could handle, even look forward to. But there was no way she was going to get my mind off of my episodes. Well, maybe for a while. What would happen if I got one while she was with me? Would she deny it then like she did the first one? Would she think, like me, that I was losing my mind?

\*    \*    \*

A Frisbee hit the beach sand next to me and rolled to a stop against my right foot.

"Sorry," said a tanned blonde in a skimpy bikini as she came running up. She bent over and picked up the Frisbee, her bikini top struggling to contain her large breasts. She glanced up and caught me looking. She smiled and ran away.

Chrissy cleared her throat. "Mmmm, get a good look?"

"What was I supposed to do? If she's gonna flaunt 'em in my face, I'll look. I wouldn't want to offend her by ignoring her, would I?"

"I doubt if she'd get offended if you didn't notice them."

"She might. I'm just trying to be polite."

"In that case, you've been polite to every woman on

the beach. I'm surprised your tongue isn't dragging in the sand."

I smiled. "You've got to admit, the view is pretty good, isn't it?"

She eyed a tanned, muscular guy with a surf board as he walked past. "Yeah, not bad. Not bad at all."

I laughed.

I felt great. We boarded Sadie last night and took off for San Diego early this morning. We'd spent most of the day on the beach. So far, I hadn't had an episode . . . not yet. But that in itself didn't mean much. They weren't consistent. I feared another one could happen at any time.

However, being on the beach had taken my mind off the episodes, at least somewhat off them. Every time I found myself thinking about an episode, I forced myself to think about something else. I didn't want to deal with them at all.

I enjoyed the water, sand, and salty breeze, but at the same time, I wasn't sure I'd be able to spend Sunday morning sitting around and doing nothing until it was time to leave for home. I liked to be working, doing something with my hands. Besides, the beach was so crowded, I was feeling a little claustrophobic with people on us on both sides. I wasn't used to having so many people so close to me, not to mention the screaming kids, bickering spouses, and rambunctious teens.

"Do you want to go in the water again?" Chrissy asked, looking at me over her sunglasses. Loose strands of her auburn hair floated in the breeze from under her pink sun visor. She looked perfect in her two-piece swimsuit.

"No, not really."

"Are you hungry? It's close to noon. We could eat if you want to."

"Sure, that sounds good." I knew she was going overboard trying to keep my mind off my episodes. If we did everything she suggested, I'd be so tired I'd sleep for a week when we got home.

She opened the picnic basket and handed me a wrapped sandwich.

As I unwrapped the plastic, a seagull dive-bombed me trying to snatch the sandwich out of my hand. "Damn, brave buggers, aren't they?" I said, watching the seagull bank into a turn. Apparently, it was going to come back for a second try at the food.

Chrissy held her sandwich close to her body. "They must do this a lot. I'll bet nobody ever does anything to scare them away, so they get braver and braver."

The gray-haired man sitting on a beach towel next to me said, "They're just a part of being at the beach. Keep a close eye out while you're eating and put your food away when you're done."

"Good advice," I said, feeling annoyed he'd heard our conversation and felt the need to interject his opinion into it.

Chrissy didn't feel the same way I did about people jumping into a private conversation. She leaned over me and said to the man, "You and your wife must come here a lot."

"Every weekend, unless the weather's bad. Our family has been doing it for forty years now," he boasted. "Course, the kids have moved away so it's just me and the wife now."

"Forty years?" I replied. "I'm having a hard time and it's only been one day."

"Why are you having a hard time?" he asked.

"Probably all the people," I said. "I'm not used to this many people around me."

"La Jolla Shores is a pretty popular beach," he offered. "But there are others that aren't as busy."

"Really?" Chrissy asked. "Where are they?"

"Depends on what you're looking for. The least busy

beach is probably Blacks Beach. It's hard to get to it though. You have to walk two miles that way." He pointed north toward a long rocky-looking beach. "Or you can park at the Hang Glider Port and walk down a steep trail."

"That doesn't sound so bad," I said. "We're in pretty good shape. A hike wouldn't be that bad." I looked at Chrissy. "Maybe we should try that beach tomorrow morning."

The man's frail-looking wife spoke up for the first time. "Tell them what kind of beach it is, Norman."

"Do I have to?"

"Yes, you need to tell them," she insisted.

"What does she mean?" Chrissy asked. "How could a beach be different?"

"The beach is not different. It's the people on the beach," Norman said. "Blacks Beach is a nude beach."

My eyebrows shot up. *Yeah, that would have been quite a surprise.* It sounded interesting though. "A nude beach? For real? Women running around with—"

"Don't even think about it," Chrissy stated emphatically. "You have a hard time keeping your eyes off the women here. You'd end up with whiplash on a nude beach."

"You got to admit," I said, "it would definitely take my mind off of my episodes."

"So would the Natural History Museum," she stated flatly.

Norman exchanged a worried look with his wife. "Episodes? You aren't infectious or anything are you?"

"No, nothing like that," I quickly said. "I've been having some strange feelings lately. We came to San Diego to get away for the weekend. We were hoping a change of setting would help."

Norman's wife sat up and gave me her full attention. "What kind of feelings are you having? I'm a nurse and

I'm curious."

I explained everything about the funny feelings I'd had and what I'd done about them.

"Sounds to me like allergies," she said. "Our youngest was allergic to everything. He had all kinds of strange things going on with his body."

Chrissy said to her, "That's what I told him, but do you think he'd listen to me?"

"NO!" both women shouted together, then laughed.

Norman rolled his eyes and shook his head. "Women."

I smiled. And felt an episode coming on.

It felt like someone was tickling my back with a feather. I tried reaching my hand over my shoulder to scratch my back, but I couldn't reach back far enough. The spot was right between my shoulder blades. I didn't want to say anything to Chrissy, but it was starting to really bother me. I squirmed around and shrugged my shoulders trying to get the feeling to stop.

I was about to lie down on my towel and use it to rub my back, when I heard a woman say, "Adam, quit tickling that man with that seagull feather."

I whipped around to see a grinning redheaded freckled toddler holding a feather in his pudgy, sand-covered hand.

"Sorry," his mom said, picking him up. "He's such a handful."

"No problem," I replied.

*Whew.* I was so happy I wasn't having another episode. All I needed was one to occur on a public beach with hundreds of people watching me. That would be disastrous. Maybe, as Chrissy had suggested, we would do the museum tomorrow morning after all.

# Chapter 8

## White Plains, NY

Hilary sat gloomily in the recliner, depressed that nothing was changing. Despite Gregory's previous momentary responses, he still lay in a coma. He'd been at the nursing home two weeks now.

She had come in early this morning to make up for the time she had missed with Gregory over the weekend. She felt a little guilty because she had not visited him since Friday.

The big New York gala for the homeless had been going on and all the socialites were expected to be in attendance, making their annual contributions and getting their photos taken by the media. She had to stay overnight in New York City, and she felt Gregory would understand that it was important for her to be there and represent the family and the company. She'd purchased the perfect dress for the occasion months before and it would have been a shame to let it sit in her closet unused. She secretly relished all the attention she got from the VIP wives, sympathizing with her over Gregory's serious condition.

But now, the reality of his condition was hitting her hard and depressing her. The nursing-home staff had reported no noticeable changes or movements in Gregory at all over the weekend. Frustrated by his deep sleep, she found herself occasionally poking, pinching, pounding on him, and prodded him with nudges when no one was around. No matter what she did, he didn't react.

She also tried being gentle, brushing his hair again, stroking his cheeks. Nothing worked. *Damn, Gregory, you are being so selfish, lying there and being pampered by the nurses and therapists instead of getting on with your real business. There are people who need you.*

Throughout the long day, disturbing thoughts worked their way into her mind as she sat with him. She realized how little she really knew him. He had always been busy with his company, with his business associates, or handling the affairs at home with the children. Her time was consumed with her volunteer work, her friends, her social engagements, and her contributions to the community.

She couldn't remember the last time they'd made love. She couldn't even remember the last time they'd taken a trip together. True, they ate dinner together most nights, but they didn't talk about anything important or meaningful. It was mainly an opportunity to sit down and eat, then go their separate ways in the house for the evening.

Hilary decided she felt fine with that. Maybe she didn't really love Gregory the way other people experienced love, but theirs was a kind of *mature* love that accepted things the way they were. They had a decent financial and social arrangement that both of them benefited from.

Divorces were messy. She'd seen too many of them among her friends, women who'd lost everything, even if their husbands were at fault for initiating the divorce. It made both spouses look bad to their families, friends, and social groups. Hilary was determined that would never happen to her. It wasn't anything she would ever allow herself to ponder.

Staring at Gregory, lying impassively on the bed, she shivered at the thought that she might have to go on alone at some point. She had not admitted it to anyone, but she was getting scared.

Immediately, she stood up and shook herself, pushing the idea out of her mind.

\* \* \*

Late afternoon finally arrived as the western sun streamed through the window. Hilary had asked Eric if she could give Gregory a sponge bath that evening, something that might give her another chance to see if she could get him to wake up.

Eric had whole-heartedly agreed.

Feeling antsy and wanting to get on with it, Hilary notified the nurse to bring in the bath water.

A tall nurse entered the room and rolled in a cart with a pan of warm water, a washcloth, and a couple of towels.

"You can leave now," Hilary rudely told the nurse. "Please close the door. I do not want to be bothered for at least an hour."

The nurse gave her a salute and closed the door.

*Where does Eric find these ill-mannered nurses?* Hilary thought as she pulled the sheet and blanket down to Gregory's feet. He wore a white hospital gown over his slender body. She decided it might be too much effort to try to roll him over and remove the gown, especially with the tube in one of his arms, so she lifted the gown as close to his shoulders as she could.

Seeing him nude for the first time in how-many-years was longer than she cared to admit. Her face flushed. She felt like she was somehow in the wrong for seeing her husband this way.

Shrugging it off, she dipped the washcloth in the warm water and started washing Gregory's upper chest. Moving from his chest down, she let her mind wander as she gently rubbed his skin. She occasionally checked to see if there were any movements anywhere on his body.

When she got to his stomach, he squirmed and started to roll from side to side.

It caught her off-guard at first. *He's moving. Is he trying to get away from me?* she wondered. *Wait, now I remember. He was always ticklish in that area.* She decided to try tickling him to keep the response going. Placing her fingernails on his stomach, she lightly drug them across the skin of his lower abdomen and sides.

Gregory jerked away, trying to escape the tickling.

Thrilled at his reaction and hoping he might be able to hear, too, Hilary asked, "Gregory? Can you hear me?" She kept tickling him, and he kept pulling away.

Hilary suddenly thought she heard him mumble something. Bending over and placing her ear next to his mouth, she kept her fingers moving on his stomach.

Gregory mumbled again, saying something that sounded like, "No . . . Chr . . ." Other words were not clear.

"What is it?" Hilary demanded. "What are you trying to say?" She stood up, filled with a mixture of elation and frustration. "You spoke. I know you are waking up. Damn, I wish the doctor was in the building. Eric is gone for the night, too, and he wouldn't give me his home phone. I'm not calling in a nurse. I don't trust any of them. They don't believe me."

She turned on Gregory with anger and began to rub the washcloth harshly over his skin again. "Why don't you respond like this when the doctor is here? No one believes me that you are trying to tell me something, trying to communicate. Why can't you work with me?"

She ran the cloth across Gregory's legs and feet. She

toweled him off.

By this time, he had stopped moving around, lying totally inert.

After pulling his gown back over his body and pulling the covers over him, she sat on the recliner. "I know you're coming back to me, Gregory, so hurry up. I'm tired of all this. I'm tired of the aggravations of working with this place. I'm tired of your father calling to know if you are going to go back to work. I'm tired of having to put on a show of being the good wife and having to visit every day. I'm missing important social engagements. When will this be over? I want my life back the way it was before your accident. Surely, you must want that, too. Aren't you tired of just lying here and doing nothing?"

There was a knock at the door.

Hilary sighed. "Come in," she called out as she stood up.

"Is everything okay?" a male nurse asked, moving toward the bed.

"Yes, everything's just fine. I finished his bath, so you can take the bath water away." She picked up her purse and strutted out of the room.

Despite her anger at Gregory for turning her life upside-down, she felt a sense of smug delight as she thought back to the sponge bath.

*Gregory spoke to me. He's going to come out of the coma. Everything is going to go back to normal. I don't care what anyone else says.* She just hoped he would come out of it soon.

# Chapter 9

## Lake Havasu City, AZ

The trip to San Diego had been great and passed without incident. I hadn't had an episode in four days. I was beginning to think the trip was what I'd needed to get rid of them. Everything was going fine.

I finished work early on Monday afternoon. Chrissy was able to leave work early, too. Wanting to take advantage of the situation to be together, we sat on my couch watching a movie.

Suddenly, out of the blue, I had another episode. It was a strange one. It felt like someone was running a warm wet cloth up and down my chest and stomach. At first, I tried to ignore it, hoping it was something that would pass, but the feeling was so real, I didn't do a very good job hiding it.

Chrissy leaned away from me and looked from my belly to my face. "You got ants in your pants or something?"

I giggled.

Chrissy tipped her head and smiled at me. "It wasn't that funny."

"No, I . . . " I giggled again, longer this time.

Sadie lifted her head and looked at me. Not seeing food or any reason to come to me, she lay back down.

"What is your problem tonight? Did you breathe some

funny dust at work today?"

I squirmed away from her and kept giggling. In between giggles, I said, "I'm having another—" Giggle. "Episode."

My hands rubbed against my stomach and sides. I pulled at my shirt, trying to get rid of the tickling feeling.

Sadie lifted her head. Her dark brown eyes watched me intently. She had to be wondering what was going on.

Chrissy sat up, serious now. Other than my very first episode, this was the only other episode she'd witnessed, and she seemed to be aware it was an episode. She shut the TV off. "What does this one feel like?"

"Right now, it feels like someone is tickling me with their fingernails, running them lightly across my skin. No. Stop." I ripped off my shirt and dug at my skin. "Chrissy, make it stop! It's so real, I . . . I . . . "

The tickling stopped. I thought it was over until the feeling of the wet cloth ran across my stomach again. To add to my distress, I could hear the voice, faint and distant. Like before, I thought it was someone outside, but the voice seemed to be coming from nowhere and everywhere at the same time. I couldn't quite make out the words. "Do you hear that?" I asked.

Chrissy cocked an ear, listening. "What? All I hear is you moving around."

"A voice," I said. "A woman's voice."

Hesitantly, Chrissy looked around the room. "Are you sure you're hearing a voice. Maybe it's—"

"No, Chrissy, wait a minute," I said, holding up my hand. "She's saying . . . something about a doctor, something about not responding. . . wait . . . she's talking about how no one believes her."

She scooted away from me. "Brad, you're scaring me. I don't like this."

I held my hand up again. "Just give me a minute, please?" It was hard concentrating on the voice with the sensations still moving across my skin. I had a feeling the voice was important, a key to what was going on, so I forced myself to concentrate on what it was saying.

Chrissy slid a little further away, her eyes wide with concern.

"Now she's talking about someone not working with her."

The voice stopped. I wasn't sure if the woman stopped talking or if I just couldn't hear her anymore. Whichever it was, I was glad that part was over. Now, if the wet cloth bit would end. It was now going across my hip and down my right leg. While not as disturbing as the tickling, it was still annoying. When it stopped, I mentally checked my body, looking for further funny feelings. When a minute passed, I was pretty sure the episode was over.

I took a deep breath and looked at Chrissy. "Sorry." I rubbed my hand across my face and through my hair. "But that was intense."

"Brad, did you really hear a voice?" Chrissy asked leaning forward, staring intently into my eyes. She still looked scared.

I pondered it for a second. "Yes, I did. It was like, it was, I don't know, coming from everywhere. It's hard to explain."

Chrissy got up and walked across the room. She got to the kitchen door and came back. Stopping in front of me, she said, "I'm not sure what's happening to you, but I do know that I love you." She lifted her hands in a what-can-I-do gesture. "And because I love you, I want you to go see a doctor. These *episodes* are getting weirder. Now, you're hearing voices, and to tell you the truth, I'm really concerned about you."

"Believe me, I'm concerned for me, too. And I agree with you about seeing a doctor. In fact, I've already got an appointment set up for tomorrow morning."

"Is this with your regular medical doctor?"

"Yeah."

She gave me an apologetic shrug and grimaced. "Maybe you should make an appointment with a psychiatrist, too."

I reached my hand up to her and she took it in hers. Gently pulling her down beside me, I said, "I'll call and make an appointment first thing tomorrow."

# Chapter 10

The next day, as Hilary entered Gregory's room, Eric came rushing in from the hallway. By the excitement on his face, Hilary knew something had alerted him about Gregory's condition to prove her right.

"Hilary, I have great news," Eric blurted. "Gregory showed some positive signs of recovery this morning. When the doctor pricked his big toe, Gregory kicked out hard with his foot. The doctor took that to be a good indication that it was more than a muscle spasm." Eric paused. "Unfortunately, he broke the doctor's hand."

A small smirk slipped out on Hilary's face. She wanted to laugh out loud, but she kept her joy of being avenged to herself. "I told you he was coming out of his coma, Eric. But neither you nor the doctor would believe me. Now, does the doctor have any idea how long it will be until he'll be completely out of his coma?"

He shook his head and spoke in a more timid tone, "You know he can't predict that, Hilary. It'll have to be on Gregory's own time when he comes out of it."

Hilary gave him a disapproving look, then glanced at Gregory, lying still in bed. She couldn't help it, but it amused her to think he kicked the old doctor and broke his hand.

Eric continued. "I'm still going to remind you that it

could be a while before we see anything more. Every coma patient is different and there is no way to tell how long any one of them will take. What's exciting about Gregory right now is that he made a sturdy kick this morning, and that's not something we've seen before. We just have to watch to see how things will play out."

"Well," Hilary stated smugly as she looked at Eric, "I want you to know that while I gave Gregory a sponge bath last night, he spoke to me."

Eric's eyes widened and his mouth dropped open. "He spoke? What did he say?"

"He was having a hard time forming words, but he was definitely trying to tell me something. His body responded to my tickling, too, just like he used to do when we were younger. I've been trying to tell you all this time that he responds to me, but you won't listen. Maybe now that the doctor got awakened with a kick, he'll believe me, too."

"Maybe you are right," Eric conceded. "If Gregory was trying to speak, that's new. It means that things are changing with him."

"You should have someone with him more often now," Hilary said. "He could wake up at any time. He shouldn't be alone."

Eric hesitated in his typical indecisiveness. "I admit these are good signs, and I have hope for more changes in the future, but right now, I'll just have the nurses look in on him a little more often."

"I don't care what you think," Hilary snapped. "Gregory is regaining his consciousness. It's going to be soon, too. I'm paying you big bucks to take care of him. If you can't afford to have someone with him more often, I'll have my attorney complain to the Better Business Bureau and the medical board about this place."

Eric put up his hands in surrender. "No, no. We can do it, Hilary. I'll see to it that someone is assigned to his room for all hours."

"Except when I'm here," she added. "The nurse can take a break while I'm visiting." She intended to show up more often, making sure everything was in order. Plus, she knew that she was the main catalyst in getting reactions from Gregory, so it was important she continue to be by his side. "I'm going to be spending more time here," she said to Eric. "I'm the one most likely to help encourage him to come back."

A slight disappointment registered in Eric's eyes. "Fine, Hilary, whatever you want."

"Now, if you don't mind, I'd like to be alone with my husband."

As Eric left the room, Hilary took Gregory's hand. She held it to her cheek while she brushed the other hand across his forehead. "Damn it, Gregory, you're almost here. I can feel it. Come on, I'm waiting for you. Please, hurry back to me so I don't have to deal with these people anymore."

# Chapter 11

## Lake Havasu City, AZ

As luck would have it, I had another episode while I was sitting in the doctor's office. The nurse had taken me into the back and recorded my weight and taken my temperature. She stuck me in an exam room and told me the doctor would be with me shortly. As I waited, I nervously studied the charts on the wall.

Doctor Ort, a middle-aged, stern-looking man stormed in a few minutes later, white coat billowing behind him with his stethoscope comfortably ensconced around his neck. Picking up my chart, he looked at it and said, "Okay . . . Brad, what is it we can do for you today?"

I took a deep breath. How was I going to tell someone, especially a doctor, that I had been having funny feelings and hearing voices? I was sure he would think I was crazy and commit me to an insane asylum immediately.

Still, I knew I had to get to the bottom of my problems, so I started with my first episode and told him everything. He nodded a few times, pursed his lips, and gave me an oh-really look. When he started writing notes on my chart, I was sure he thought I was crazy.

As I finished my story, I felt someone take my left hand and hold it. Fingers brushed across my face. I rubbed my hand while I shook my head back and forth.

"Is something wrong?" Doctor Ort asked. "You seem to be upset suddenly."

"Yeah . . . I'm . . . I'm having an episode."

His eyes narrowed. "What's happening. Talk to me."

I decided to go for broke and explained everything that was happening. "It feels like someone is rubbing my face, and squeezing my hand. And I can hear a voice."

"Is the voice a man or woman? What is it saying?"

"It's a woman. She's saying, 'You're almost here. Come on, I'm waiting for you.'" I was amazed at how clear the voice had become. Like the woman was close enough that I could hear her, but far enough away that I couldn't see her. I rubbed at my face, knowing full well it wouldn't help, but I needed to do something.

"Is that all she said?"

"She said, 'Please hurry back to me.' "

"Oookay," he said as he wrote more on my chart.

"It's over," I said, slumping in relief on the chair. "It's done."

"Do you take any medications, Brad?"

"No, nothing."

"Drink?"

"An occasional beer."

"Illegal drugs?"

"No, of course not."

"How about natural medications, herbs, vitamins, that kind of thing?"

"No, nothing. I've even been keeping track of what I eat and when I eat it. As far as I can tell, I haven't done anything different than I've always done."

"And you say these . . . episodes . . . are getting more intense?"

"Yeah, each one seems to be more intense than the one before. I'm afraid one day I'll start seeing whoever's talking." I chuckled, even though it was something that really concerned me.

"Yes, that would seem to be a logical progression, wouldn't it?" He paused for a moment. "Brad, to be honest with you, I'm not sure what, if anything is going on with you." He held up a hand to forestall my imminent question. "I don't think your problem is medically related. That said, I think you'd be better off talking to someone who specializes in—" He smiled at me. "—these types of cases."

"You mean like a shrink?"

He nodded. "I'm going to refer you to a good friend of mine. I'm sure he'll be able to help you figure out what is going on in that mind of yours."

*Yup, he thinks I'm wackier than a fruitcake.* "Actually, I already have an appointment with Doctor Holden," I said. "I wasn't sure if you'd be able to help me, so I called this morning and made an appointment. Lucky for me they had a cancelation and were able to fit me in tomorrow morning."

"Good, that's great. I know him, He's a good doctor. In the meantime, I'd like to run some standard blood tests, maybe do an MRI and CT scan, just to make sure there's nothing medically that could be causing these halluci . . . these episodes."

Resigned to the fact that I was now going to be put through the ringer, I nodded. "Sure, doc, whatever you need to do. I just want to get to the bottom of it."

"I'll have my nurse give you the information about the tests I want to run and schedule you for them." He got up and slipped out the door.

"Great," I said to the empty room. "Just great."

# Chapter 12

## White Plains, NY

The next day, Gregory continued to respond to Hilary's physical touch and presence. She grew more and more convinced that he was on the verge of coming out of his coma. In fact, she'd become an obsessed woman, spending the whole day at the nursing home, wanting to be there when he woke up. She neglected things at home and in her social circle as well as refused to take any more calls from Gregory's father. She told his father outright not to call any more about Gregory. She would call *him*.

She'd come in early to sit with Gregory. For some reason, she had a feeling that this would be the day. She'd gotten there while the doctor was making his rounds with his left hand in a cast. Even though the doctor made her no promises about Gregory's recovery, he agreed that Gregory was showing good signs of improvement.

The male nurse poked his head into the room. "Would you like anything?" he asked.

"No, I'm good." Hilary was glad Eric finally switched nurses and assigned this male nurse to Gregory for the daytime hours. This nurse was much more aware of her wants and needs. He was always in the room when she arrived and returned to the room when she left.

Hilary took Gregory's hand. "The children are doing the same as usual," she said. "Brittany is flitting around with her loser friends. Jonathan can't settle down in any direction. I told your father to stop calling me, and I haven't heard from him since. I saw your mother's picture in the high-society paper. She's been working in an orphanage and contributing large sums of money."

She squeezed his hand and hoped that, if Gregory heard her talking about familiar things, he might wake up. "William told me that you and your father have been working on a new business deal. He didn't give me the details, but he was excited that it would make us a lot of money. They're still worried, though, that they will lose the three-million-dollar startup business you initiated."

Gregory's breathing started becoming more rapid. His eyes moved under his eyelids.

*He's understanding what I'm saying*, she thought. *He wants to respond but he can't.* She squeezed his hand hard. "Damn it, Gregory, come on. I know you're on your way back, but I'm tired of waiting. Come back. Today. Now."

His eyes shot open wide. He jerked his hand out of hers and yelled, "No!"

Frightened at his force, Hilary jumped up and let out a small scream. She staggered toward the door in alarm. "Nurse," she called, keeping an eye on Gregory.

He sat up bone-stiff in his bed, gasping for breath, looking around, his eyes wide with terror.

In shock, she ran from the room toward the nurses' station. *Did Gregory respond to my demands? Did he really tell me no?* As ecstatic as she felt that he'd responded with such life in him, she was scared to go back into the room alone. *He might be dangerous until he realizes where he is and that he is okay.*

At the nurses' desk, the male nurse was conversing with Gregory's former nurse and a younger nurse with her long red hair pulled up into a bun.

"Quick," Hilary shouted, stammering the words out. "Go to Gregory's room. He's sitting up, talking, and thrashing around."

All three nurses stared at her in silence, not grasping the seriousness of what she was saying.

"Go! Hurry," she demanded, "before he hurts himself."

The male nurse took off down the hall toward Gregory's room.

"I'll let Mr. Bolanger know," said the overweight nurse, picking up a phone and punching numbers.

The redhead quickly ran down the hall. "I'll help with Gregory."

Hilary followed her. "It's about time somebody moved fast around here."

# Chapter 13

## Lake Havasu City, AZ

I sat in my car in the parking lot of a medical building. I had just left the office of the psychiatrist after my first appointment. Yesterday when I had explained what was going on with me, his secretary had gotten me in today. It was a good thing, too. I was having multiple episodes, starting from the time I'd left Doctor Ort's office yesterday. I'd left a job early and went home because I couldn't function adequately. Each episode seemed a little more real and more intense than the last. Although I felt I was handling them okay, I feared I was going crazy.

Doctor Holden had been nice enough to listen to my story and show interest, but I sensed he thought I was just another nut case, making it all up. I don't know. Maybe he was right. Maybe all this was just in my head. Maybe I was going crazy. It sure felt real when it was happening. I didn't know what to think anymore.

Chrissy had been very supportive, helpful in every way. She did research on the internet, looking for people who had similar experiences. She found a blog where people talked about their own *episodes* and compared them with each other, but none of them seemed to be quite like mine. We suspected most of them were dreams or made up in their imaginations.

I laid my head on the steering wheel. So far today, I hadn't had an episode, but I found myself constantly on edge that it could happen at any time. I didn't want to go home. I didn't want to call one of my clients and start a job, knowing I wouldn't be able to concentrate on the work. Instead, I decided to go for a drive.

I headed north out of town on Highway 95. I figured I'd drive to the truck stop at I-40 and get a cup of coffee. I needed to be alone for a while and think things through. Chrissy would probably be curious what happened in the doctor's office, but I didn't want to talk to her just now.

Traffic was light and my mind drifted as I mulled over what Doctor Holden and I had talked about. Mostly, he let me do all the talking and he offered little advice. He asked me questions about my home life, my work, my health, my sleeping habits. He said he could write me a prescription, but I didn't want to be on drugs. I didn't think they would help if an episode began. As far as I could see, the doctor didn't help me at all other than to suggest I come back for another appointment in a week.

Driving along and daydreaming, not paying much attention, I suddenly felt someone take a hold of my hand and squeeze hard. As clear as if the woman was sitting right next to me, I heard her say, "Damn it, Gregory, come on. I know you are on your way back, but I'm tired of waiting. Come back today. Now."

I got so caught up in this latest episode, I wasn't paying attention to my surroundings. I didn't see, until the last minute, an oncoming car drifting into my lane.

I yanked the steering wheel hard to the right and yelled, "*No!*" At the same time, I slammed on the brakes.

It was too late. I couldn't stop what was about to happen.

# Chapter 14

## White Plains, NY

The redheaded nurse was closing the door to Gregory's room as Hilary came up behind her. Hilary shoved it open and barreled into the room. She slid to a stop next to the nurse.

Gregory was now lying down, his eyes wide open with panic as he looked around the room frantically. He seemed frightened by the nurses and even by Hilary's presence. It was clear he didn't know where he was.

The male nurse stood by the bed looking at Gregory in astonishment as if he didn't know what to do.

"Why aren't you helping him?" Hilary asked as she stayed by the redheaded nurse near the door. She feared Gregory might jump up and attack her. "Can't you calm him down?"

"Not sure *what* to do," the male nurse blurted. "Don't want to hurt him."

Fuming that the nurses weren't doing anything, Hilary rolled her eyes, *Can't they hire anyone with brains in this place?* "Gregory," she said calmly, stepping forward tentatively, "I'm here. It's okay, I'm right here." She got close enough to the bed to touch his hand.

He jerked it away from her and his body thrashed around as if he was trying to get away from something.

The male nurse locked down the arm that held the IV.

Hilary tried again to calm Gregory with her voice, but he started throwing his free arm around and she was afraid he would hit her. Backing off, all she could do was watch and hope that he didn't hurt himself.

Eric and the overweight nurse rushed into the room.

"My god, what's happening to him?" Eric blurted as he stared in shock at Gregory.

"I don't know," said the male nurse, holding down Gregory's arm and backing up to give the overweight nurse more room to attend to him.

"I ain't never seen nothin' like this," replied the former nurse.

"I think he's finally out of his coma," Hilary stated as she hesitantly moved closer, behind the nurse.

"We've never had any coma patient react like this," Eric said in a tone of amazement. "Normally, they wake up slowly, taking hours or even days to become fully awake. This is extraordinary!"

"Well, do something," Hilary demanded. "He's going to hurt himself if you don't help him." It upset her that Eric was more interested in the clinical aspect of Gregory's situation than in helping him.

"Yes, we should make sure he doesn't hurt himself." Eric spoke to the overweight nurse. "Go get a sedative. And hurry." To the redhead, who stood by the door all this time, he said, "We need two strong orderlies. Go get Marcus and Bart. Tell them to hurry."

"Yes, doctor." She ducked out the door.

Hilary was about to ask Eric why he had sent for orderlies when he had three perfectly good nurses standing in the room, but Gregory started mumbling words as he thrashed around.

"Is he trying to talk?" Eric asked, his eyes wide in disbelief. He made sure he stayed clear of the bed.

In a whisper that Hilary could barely hear, Gregory said, "Chrissy, I'm . . . "

*Chrissy? Who is Chrissy?* Hearing her husband say another woman's name the first thing out of his mouth inflamed Hilary with a jealous anger. Not caring about her safety, she surged forward and grabbed Gregory's free-flailing arm. Struggling to keep him from hitting her, she shook him, demanding, "Who is Chrissy?"

Gregory struggled to sit partway up. "No, no, no . . . Chrissy . . . please . . . I love . . . "

The overweight nurse rushed into the room with a syringe. While the male nurse struggled to hold Gregory's arm still for the shot, the woman stuck the needle in his arm.

Suddenly, Gregory collapsed onto the bed, his arms flopping to his side as if his muscles had been cut.

The door banged open and two muscular male orderlies rushed into the room. Their eyes flew from person to person, looking for an obvious problem. With nothing apparently wrong, one of them said, "What do you need?"

"Nothing now," Eric calmly stated. He motioned to the male nurse to check Gregory's eyes.

When the nurse lifted Gregory's eyelids, Gregory turned his head and weakly pushed the man's hand away.

"It looks like he's coming out of his coma," Eric stated excitedly. To the staff, he said, "I am scheduling someone to be in this room at all times. Except when his wife is here, of course." He nodded at Hilary. "All of you should be on alert, in case we need you again."

Still inflamed over who the hell Chrissy was and whether or not Gregory loved her, Hilary almost missed the fact that Eric was now agreeing with her that Gregory was coming out of his coma. *What an idiot*, she thought.

Then and there, she decided that she was going to live in that room with Gregory until he was awake enough to answer a few questions she had for him.

# Chapter 15

I slowly awakened, coming out of a deep sleep, deeper than I'd ever had. I struggled to open my eyes. I could hear someone moving round nearby.

"Gregory? Gregory, can you hear me?"

It was a woman's voice, fairly faint, one that seemed vaguely familiar. *Was she talking to me? Why was she calling me Gregory?* I felt someone take my hand and rub the back of it. I wondered if this was one of my funny feelings. I jerked my hand away and the feeling stopped.

Finally, I forced my eyes open.

The woman swam into a blurry focus.

"Wh . . . where am I?" I croaked.

The woman gasped. Then she cried. "Oh, Gregory, you don't know how happy I am to hear your voice." She took my hand again and held it so tight I couldn't get it out of her grasp, hard as I tried.

"Who . . . who are you?"

A strange look crossed her face as the tears subsided. "I'm your wife, silly. Don't you recognize me?"

*Wife? Wow, this is too much.* I drifted into blackness.

\* \* \*

The next time I woke up, I looked around and saw nobody in the room. I was pretty sure it was night. The curtains on the window were closed with no apparent light coming through them. The lights in the room had been dimmed.

I studied the room a little closer. It looked like a hospital room with a TV hanging on the wall, a tray on wheels near the bed with a pitcher of water and plastic cups, a door leading into what was probably a bathroom. The nightstand next to the bed held a phone and TV remote. The stand was made of polished oak. Across the way, there was a matching dresser with white linens on top. The dresser seemed out of place for a hospital room.

I noticed a large Lazy-Boy recliner on one side of the bed. To my surprise, I realized that someone was sleeping in it: a woman.

The memory of a dream came to me of a woman claiming to be my wife. Maybe I was still dreaming. I struggled to remember why I was here. What had happened to land me in a room like this?

An IV fluid bag hung near the bed with a line to my right arm. No doubt, this was a hospital.

Lying still, I did a quick assessment of my body. Nothing seemed to hurt. I lifted the blanket to see a flimsy hospital gown reaching down to my thighs. *Okay. Note to self. Don't get up if there's anybody else in the room.*

I moved my legs and arms. Nothing hurt, but I felt weak. Other than the IV, I didn't have any bandages anywhere on my body, as far as I could tell. Other than the IV in my arm, only a catheter was connected to my body. I patted every part of my head with my hand to see if there were any dressings or bandages there, but I found nothing. Nothing that would explain why I was in a hospital.

I saw the call button hanging from the side rail on the bed and thought about pushing it for a nurse, but for some reason, I didn't want to wake up the woman sleeping in the recliner.

I pulled the sheets up to my neck. Doing a quick inventory of my body again, I realized I felt fine, maybe a little tired and weak. I decided I would get up in the morning, call Chrissy, and go home.

* * *

I woke up to the sound of a flushing toilet. I opened my eyes, looking around. Daylight streamed through the cracks of the curtains, so I assumed it was morning.

I'd had a good night's sleep. I felt great, ready to get up for the day. First, I'd have to have help with the IV.

Remembering the toilet flushing, my quick glance confirmed the bathroom door was shut. *Who is in there?* A crumpled-up blanket and a pillow had been thrown on the Lazy-Boy recliner.

Before I could contemplate it further, the door opened and a woman walked out.

Her brunette hair, cut in a short stylish fashion, set off her high cheekbones and beautiful face. Her wrinkled blue-linen suit looked expensive. She wore diamond stud earrings and a diamond pendant on a necklace around her neck. On her left-hand ring finger, she strutted one of the largest diamonds I'd ever seen. As she walked across the room, she carried herself with confidence, and maybe a little haughtiness.

She didn't seem to notice that I was awake, but I certainly noticed that she was the woman in my dream, the one claiming we were married. I knew one thing for sure, there was no way I could be her husband. Not that she was anyone I would even be interested in. She obviously lived a lifestyle I never knew. I could never afford a rock like that.

She looked up. "Oh, Gregory, you're awake." She rushed to my bedside.

"Yeah," I replied cautiously.

"How do you feel?" she asked, her brown eyes showing delight.

"Really good. In fact, I'd like to get up. Can you help me?" I was about to throw the covers off when I remembered what I was wearing. Hospital gowns don't cover much, not to mention the fact that I still had a catheter in me. I settled back down. "On second thought," I said, holding up a hand, "can you get a nurse to help me?"

She reached over and pressed the nurse-call button on the side rail of my bed.

I reached out and pushed the button to raise the back of the bed. I held the button until it had me in an almost upright position.

Tears formed in the woman's eyes. "I can't tell you how happy I am that you've finally came out of your coma, Gregory. From the first week you were here, I told Eric you were going to wake up, but he didn't believe me. No one believed me, not the nurses and not even the doctor. They tried to tell me your responses to all my touches were just random movements." She wiped a tear from her cheek. "I've got so many things to tell you. I'm glad you want to get up. You'll be back to the company in no time."

Needless to say, I was completely confused. "First of all, why do you keep calling me Gregory? My name is Brad. And who is Eric?"

"*Brad*? Why would you think your name is Brad? You're Gregory. Obviously, your mind is still a little muddled. Eric Bolanger is the Executive Director of Whispering Pines Nursing Facility. You've been in a coma for three weeks and most of that time you've been here in Whispering Pines."

"I was in a coma?" Now, more than anything, I wanted to get out of bed and call Chrissy. I wished someone would hurry up and get here to disconnect me from these tubes.

A nurse with red hair walked into the room. She stopped short and put her hand to her mouth when she saw me sitting up in bed. "Oh, my. I need to get Mr. Bolanger." She turned and rushed out of the room.

I found that funny. "I guess she wasn't expecting me to be awake," I said grinning. "By the way, what's your name?"

She huffed. "Hilary. Hilary Nordmeyer."

I raised my eyebrows. "Nordmeyer?" What made her think I was her husband with a name like Nordmeyer?

"It's your name, too," she said testily. "In fact, it was your name to begin with. I only got it when we got married."

"So, according to you, I'm Greg Nordmeyer?"

"It's *Gregory* Nordmeyer."

A frazzled-looking man wearing a spiffy suit and tie swept into the room. His eyes never left mine as he covered the space between the door and a few feet from the end of my bed, seemingly not wanting to get too close. "Gregory, how are you feeling? Do you have pain anywhere? Are you dizzy? Do you—?"

"Whoa, mister, slow down before you give yourself a heart attack. I'm fine. In fact, I feel great. But I would really like to get out of bed and stand up."

He put up his palms. "In due time. The doctor needs to examine you first. I wouldn't want you to overdo it. After all, you've been in a coma for three weeks. We need to exercise a little caution here."

Unable to wrap my mind around what he'd said, I asked, "I take it you are Eric?"

"Oh, I'm sorry. Yes, you've never met me. I'm Eric

Bolanger. Your wife, Hilary," he said as he nodded his head toward my supposed wife, "had you transferred to Whispering Pines when the hospital could no longer do anything for you."

I was getting a little ticked off. "Okay, first off, Eric, my name is not Gregory. It's Brad. I don't know who this woman is, I've never seen her before in my life. What I'd like to do is make a phone call." I reached for the phone on the table next to the bed. Picking up the handset, I was surprised at how heavy it felt. I shrugged it off, blaming it on me not being active for a few days. "How do I get an outside line?"

Eric and Hilary looked at each other. Eric held up a placating hand to the woman. "He's probably confused. After all, he's been in a coma. Let's give him some time and let him do what he wants. I'm sure he'll come around pretty quick."

I was still holding the handset, wondering how they could stand there and talk about me as if I wasn't even there.

"An outside line?" I wiggled the phone back and forth, my arm starting to quiver from the weight.

"Dial 9," Eric said.

I dialed 9. When the tone came through, I entered Chrissy's cell phone number. A tone beeped and a voice said, "*I'm sorry, but you need to dial an area code to connect with that number.*"

I hung up the phone. "That's strange. It said it was long distance." Then it hit me. Of course, Lake Havasu didn't have facilities like this. I must be in Vegas or Phoenix.

While the two of them watched in curiosity, I tried again. This time the call went through.

It rang three times and a man answered. "Yo, what up?"

Hearing a male voice threw me. "Is . . . is Chrissy

there?"

"Dude, wrong number." He hung up.

"I must have dialed it wrong." I carefully redialed.

"Yo, what up?"

I slammed the phone down. Now, I was getting pissed.

Eric opened his mouth to speak, but I didn't want to hear anything he had to say.

"I don't care what you want, Eric. I'm getting out of this bed. You can either get someone to help me, or not, but it would go much easier if I could have help with the IV and the cath."

He seemed antsy, having a hard time making a decision. "Well, it looks like you will be fine without the cath and IV. I'll have a nurse remove them. The doctor should be in the building making his rounds by now. I'll have someone find him. He should examine you before we go any further."

The red-headed nurse stuck her head into the room.

"Nurse," I shouted before she could leave again. "Eric said you can take my IV and cath out. Come do it, now." I felt bad ordering her around with Eric standing there, but I had the feeling that if I didn't take control of the situation, nothing would get done.

The nurse looked at Eric, who reluctantly nodded his ascent. She smiled and winked at me as she brushed past the two of them and headed for my bed. I had the distinct feeling she was on my side and would gladly do whatever she could to spite Eric. Or maybe it was Hilary.

The nurse stood next to my bed and looked at my arm. She went to the oak dresser and checked in the first drawer. "It looks like we're out of tape and gauze and a few other things. I'll get them and be right back." She patted my arm gently.

As she headed toward the door, Eric said to her, "Ask the nurse in charge to find the doctor and have him come to this room. Also have her order some liquids for a patient who has just come out of a coma."

She nodded and quickly left.

"I need to make another phone call," I said, picking up the phone again. Eric and Hilary watched silently as I dialed.

The phone rang three times before a woman answered, but it wasn't my mother. Another wrong number. I hung up and tried my daughter with the same result. A fear in the pit of my stomach rose. Everything was wrong and I couldn't get a grip on what was happening. I hung up the phone.

From the looks on their faces, I knew Hilary and Eric were curious about the phone calls. "I tried calling my parents, my daughter, and my girlfriend, but—"

"*Girlfriend?*" Hilary demanded, a dark shadow crossing her face. "What are you talking about?"

"Remember," Eric interrupted, trying to keep Hilary calm, "he's probably confused. He may be remembering a dream and thinks those people are real. Go easy on him for a while."

"Chrissy, my daughter Megan, and my parents are real," I stated. I pinched myself. This room, these people, they have to be a dream.

"Chrissy?" Hilary barked. "You said her name before. The other day. Is she your girlfriend?" Hilary's body stiffened and her mouth got hard.

"As a matter of fact, she is," I said flatly.

Hilary's brown eyes seethed with anger, but Eric broke up the conversation. "And do all of them live here?" he asked in a soothing voice. "In White Plains?"

"White Plains? Where's that?" I asked.

"White Plains, New York," Hilary blurted.

I stopped cold. *New York*? I was becoming more and more convinced that this was a dream. I didn't see how I could be in a bed clear across the country, unless they transported me while I was in the coma. Maybe it was possible, but until I could look outside and prove it to myself that this was not the Southwest, I had to believe that I was somewhere near Havasu.

"Where do you think we are?" Eric asked.

"In Arizona. Chrissy and I live in Arizona. Megan and my parents live in Golden, Colorado."

Eric's brow furrowed in consternation. He looked at Hilary.

I immediately added, "Yeah, well, maybe I'm in Phoenix or maybe Vegas. As far as I know, Havasu doesn't have a Whispering Pines Facility."

Hilary and Eric started to speak at the same time.

"Let me handle this," Eric said. "He may be more delusional than I thought."

The nurse suddenly entered the room to take out my IV. Crossing the room, she set a few items on a rolling stand and pushed it next to my bed. "I'm gonna need you to lay your bed down flat, sweetie."

Reluctantly, I held the button down until the bed was flat. It felt horrible. I didn't want to lay down, I wanted to get up.

Pulling my blanket down, she placed her hand on my leg. Taking a handful of my gown in her hand, she glanced at Hilary and Eric. "You want to stay while I do this?"

"Oh, yes . . ." Eric said, clearing his voice. "The catheter. Come, Hilary. Let's give them some privacy. We'll be back in ten minutes." He took Hilary's arm and guided her out the door.

Surprisingly, Hilary went without an argument.

"Whew. I'm glad they're gone," the nurse said as she pulled up my nightgown and proceeded to remove my cath.

"Yeah, me, too." I was hoping they wouldn't come back soon. I wasn't going to have a lot of time, so I had to hurry. Sensing that the nurse sympathized with me, I quickly said, "I want to ask you a few questions before they come back." I hoped to keep my mind off what she was doing.

"Sorry, honey, I'm married." She smiled at me and then glanced at the closed door. "Unfortunately, so are you."

"Actually, I'm not," I replied.

She cocked her head at me and raised an eyebrow. "Do tell." She removed the cath and started removing the dressing on the IV, then the needle.

"That woman is not my wife. I've never seen her before. Let me ask you, what town are we in?"

"You feeling okay? You feeling dizzy or anything?"

"No, I'm fine, really. I just need to clear up a few things in my mind."

"Okay." She nodded. "White Plains."

"New York?"

"Yeah." She taped a piece of cotton to my arm and took a step back.

"Cool," I said looking at my arm. "Now, I can get up."

She put a restraining hand on me. "Hold on. That depends on what the doc says."

My muscles felt stiff and weak, so I took it slow, sitting all the way up and twisting my body until my legs hung off the edge of the bed. My head spun for a short moment. The movement took more out of me than I had expected. Apparently, I had been lying down longer than I thought.

"You should wait for the doctor," the nurse reminded me. "You'll get me in trouble."

I checked my arms and chest with my hands. I was shocked. I had lost quite a bit of my muscle mass. Working as hard as I did, I always stayed in pretty good shape. I could feel my ribs through the gown. My legs, too, looked thin and boney. My tan, normally very dark this time of year, was non-existent. Even if I could get to my feet, I wondered if I would be able to stand by myself.

Had I really been in a coma for three weeks? What was I doing before that, before I woke up in this room? I drew a blank. The words *funny feeling* kept popping into my mind, but I just couldn't grasp what it meant.

I put my foot on the floor to stand up, but my head reeled.

"A little weak, are we?" the nurse said, startling me.

I nodded. "Yeah."

"Okay. Don't move. You shouldn't be doing this on your on. And you should wait for the doctor, but I'll get a wheelchair, just in case. You stay right there, ya hear?" She stood with her hands on her hips and glared at me, waiting for an answer.

"Don't worry. I won't try to get up while you're gone. I don't want to hurt myself and have to extend my stay here." I waved her out of the room. "Hurry. Go."

While she was gone, I thought about the situation. I pinched myself a couple times to see if this was real. The pinches hurt. *What am I going to do next? It doesn't matter how I got here or how long I've been here, I'll deal with that stuff later. The first thing I have to do is get out of this place.*

Without getting up, I looked around for my clothes. Maybe they were in the dresser. On the other hand, if I had been transferred here straight from the hospital like Eric said, I wouldn't have had clothes on. And being in a coma, I wouldn't have had a need for clothes. *Number 1 on my list: get clothes.*

The nurse pushed a wheelchair through the open door, followed closely by Eric, Hilary, and an elderly man in a white coat with spectacles on his nose.

"Well, well, what do we have here?" the doctor said,

stepping next to me and putting his cold stethoscope on my back. "How do you feel?"

"Fine."

"Take a couple deep breaths." When he finished, he let the stethoscope drop at his chest and took a pen light and shined it in my eyes.

For some reason, this reminded me of being poked in the eye. *That funny feeling thing again.*

Hilary came closer to the bed. "I want to take him home as soon as possible."

The doctor looked at her sharply over his glasses. "I understand your situation, Mrs. Nordmeyer, but I'm not ready to release him. I need to keep him at least two or three days to make sure he doesn't have a relapse or complications."

Hilary stamped her foot on the floor. "Fine, but I'm going to come here every day until you do release him." She folded her arms across her chest and glared defiantly at him.

"That's fine, Hilary," Eric said. "We'll make sure you have as much private quality time as possible."

I cringed at the thought.

The doctor turned to the nurse. "In the meantime, he can begin drinking liquids and eating soft foods. He needs to build up his strength. The physical therapist should continue the schedule with him to help him rebuild some of his muscle mass.

"And you, sir," he said to me, "I can see you are anxious to get up and moving. Take it carefully. I don't think you are ready to try standing yet."

"I'm just feeling a little weak is all."

"That's only to be expected. You've been in that bed a while. Your muscles are not used to being used."

The nurse parked the wheelchair next to my bed. After locking the wheels in place, she and the doctor helped me stand up and then eased me into the chair.

It was a sobering experience. Not only that I needed help, but I never thought it could be so tiring to do such a little thing. By the time I got situated in the chair, my breaths came hard and I had broken out in a sweat. Not good. Not good at all. How was I going to get away from these people and back to Chrissy if I couldn't even go from a bed to a chair?

As much as I hated to admit it, it looked like I was going to have to depend on Hilary for a little while. But only long enough to gain my strength back. After that, I would be gone.

Other than Hilary, my only other option was to stay here in the nursing home. *Hey, not a bad idea.* I would get three meals a day, daily exercise, a physical therapist to help me rebuild my muscles, and I'd have a doctor and nurses available to assist me if I needed help.

*Okay, staying here is Option 1. Going with Hilary is Option 2. Maybe if I have enough time to think about it, an Option 3 will present itself.*

# Chapter 16

I awoke to sunlight filtering in between the open curtains on my window. Feeling awake and alert, I sat up and swung my legs over the bed. The movement didn't exhaust me like it had yesterday, but it made me a little dizzy and I still felt too weak to walk to the bathroom on my own. I pushed the call button.

While I waited for the nurse, I planned a course of action for the day. Obviously, Hilary would be back. That was a given. I didn't want to make her angry, but I wasn't going to spend every minute of the day with her. She'd just have to deal with it.

"Good morning, Gregory," said a male nurse as he pushed open the door.

"Good morning. And by the way, my name's Brad."

He walked to my bed. "Really? Because on your chart, it says Gregory."

My need to pee overrode my desire to argue. That would come later. "Fine. Would you please help me to the bathroom?"

"No problem . . . Gregory." He reached for the wheelchair.

"No. I want to try walking."

"Sorry, doctor's orders. For now, you have to use the wheelchair." Seeing the disappointment on my face, he added, "I'll see what I can do to get you up and walking later today."

"Great. Thanks."

He wheeled me to the bathroom. "You have to promise me you will stay sitting down to do your thing. I don't trust that you can stand long enough to get the job done."

Turns out, he was right. In the privacy of the bathroom, I tried standing on my own. I lasted almost five seconds before I had to sit again. "Small steps," I told myself. I could tell I was stronger than yesterday, so I didn't let myself worry about it. I was confident that, in a few more days, I'd be walking by myself with no problems.

The nurse wheeled me back to my bed and helped me get settled. As the nurse left, Eric came into the room.

"Eric," I said, adjusting the pillows behind my back, "before Hilary gets here, I need to talk with you."

"Okay." He sat in the recliner and crossed his legs. He arranged his pant leg so the crease laid just right. "Go ahead."

"I was serious when I told you that she isn't my wife. I've never seen her before. Everything I told you yesterday is the truth. I'm from Arizona and—"

"Gregory," he interrupted, "let's just concentrate on getting you well enough to go home. I'm sure that, as time goes by, you'll remember who you are."

Before I could respond, clicking heels sounded on the floor at the door and Hilary walked into the room in a perfectly fitted silk pantsuit with expensive-looking jewelry. So much for my private talk with Eric.

The rest of the day and the following two days were a blur of doctor visits, physical therapy treatments, improvement of my food intake, and putting up with Hilary. The therapist seemed surprised at how fast I was walking and gaining strength. He told me he'd never seen another coma patient improve so quickly. I had a strong motivation to get better. I wanted to go home.

Hilary sat by my bedside many hours each day. She constantly complained about my so-called dad pestering her to get me to come back to work now that I was out of the coma. She constantly complained about all the things she was missing in her life because I was lying in a nursing home bed. She was annoyed, as well, that I kept insisting I was Brad.

I faked being asleep most of the time. Other times, my mind tuned her out as I daydreamed of the life I wanted to get back to. As much as I tried, I couldn't convince Eric to let me stay at the nursing home instead of going home with Hilary when I was released.

\* \* \*

On the day the doctor released me, Hilary walked into my room with some clothes to wear: black Docker pants, a white, long-sleeved dress shirt, and black dress shoes

I frowned at her selection. I would have preferred jeans, a T-shirt, and sneakers. These classy clothes were way too dressy for me. They made me feel like I was going to a business meeting. Unfortunately, I had no choice, unless I wanted to strut out of the building in my hospital gown. Strangely, the clothes fit pretty well, Maybe a little loose in places.

The good news was that I was now able to walk pretty much on my own with the help of a cane and, occasionally, a walker. Another few days and I'd be rid of these, too. The bad news was that I hadn't been able to contact Chrissy, my daughter, or my parents. They had to be worried about me.

I just hoped Chrissy was going to my house and

taking care of Sadie. I hated to think of Sadie locked in the house and running out of food and water. Not to mention, the mess she'd make on the floor if she couldn't get outside to relieve herself. I needed to get strong enough to leave and get back to Arizona, or at least to Golden to stay with my parents while I recuperated completely.

It was almost one o'clock in the afternoon when I walked out the front door of Whispering Pines with Hilary. Between the wheelchair and a walker, I had been over the entire grounds several times since I had awakened in that bed. The surroundings were lush with greens and the smell of fresh-cut grass or fall blossoms often hung in the air. Being early autumn, the leaves of the trees were already turning to bright reds and golds. This was a beautiful place and what I imagined the New England states would look like. It certainly wasn't the Arizona desert. The weather was cooler here, too, although this day seemed to be the perfect temperature. I had resigned myself that, somehow, I had ended up in the state of New York.

Hilary pointed to a black limo. "That's our car."

"Our car?" I said, glancing sideways at her to see if she was joking.

"Well, our ride. The car belongs to the family trust. Any family member can use it as long as it isn't being loaned for use by someone else. I thought it would be nice to use it today."

The driver stood next to an open rear door. "Good afternoon, sir. It's good to see you again."

"Yeah, thanks," I replied as I slid onto the leather seat. The temperature of the interior was cool. A light jazz melody played through hidden speakers.

Hilary slid in the seat across from me. The driver shut the door behind her and climbed into the driver's seat. She didn't give the driver any directions, so I figured, as the family driver, he knew where she lived.

Curious, I asked, "How far is it to your—"

Hilary shot me a dirty look.

"I'm sorry. To *our* house?"

"Less than five minutes."

In five minutes, we pulled into the grass-lined circular driveway of a huge two-story house. Light gray trim around eight windows, two on each side of the front door and four above, contrasted with the pure whiteness of the house. The upper windows, probably bedrooms, were dark.

The limo pulled up to the curb at the front door and let us out. Hilary hustled me inside, as fast as she could get me to move with the cane. Maybe she was afraid I'd run away if I got the chance.

When the front door opened, the first thing that caught my eye was the floor: deep, dark, with highly polished wood. Not the laminate stuff that looks like wood. I'm talking *real* wood. They were beautiful.

The foyer continued straight ahead through the house to a set of double doors that led into the back yard. On the left side of the foyer, a floral-print carpeted staircase curved gently up to the second level. It had white banisters and a wooden handrail made of the same wood as the floor. Matching arched doorways off the foyer led to rooms on the right and the left. Hilary turned right.

I followed her through the arched door and down a short hallway to the kitchen and dining room. A set of French double doors opened out back where I could see a tiled swimming pool and lots of vegetation in the form of shrubs, bushes, and fruit trees. Being in construction, this was a house I could appreciate.

"Well, what do you think?" Hilary asked as she made a sweeping motion with her hands across the kitchen and dining room.

Various sized tiles with a wood-like pattern covered

the floor of the two rooms. The kitchen cabinets were white with silver handles. A black granite countertop matched the black and chrome of the appliances. A round wooden table with four brown chairs sat in the dining room.

"It's okay, I guess."

"Just okay?"

"No," I hurriedly replied. "It's really nice. I'm just not used to this much . . . richness."

She chuckled. "You should be. We've lived here for the last twenty-five years."

*Twenty-five years? Seems like this place would be familiar if I'd been here that long.* Curiosity got the better of me. "How much is this place worth?"

"We paid seven million twenty-five years ago. I don't know what it would sell for today, but if I had to guess, I'd say it's probably worth around ten million."

"So I take it you're . . . rich?"

"*We're* rich," she corrected.

"How rich?"

"The last time we checked, about six months ago, we had a net worth of just over one hundred million dollars."

I let out a long, almost silent whistle. "Wow."

"But since you went into the coma, it's probably dropped some. William says they have had some negotiation problems with one of the businesses you were working with, so that might have an impact on our net worth. But we'll discuss that later." She walked to the refrigerator and pulled out a Diet Coke. "Is any of this feeling familiar to you yet?"

"Nope, sorry."

She didn't offer me anything to drink. Either she wasn't in hostess mode or she figured if I wanted something, I'd get it myself. In fact, a cold drink sounded pretty good. I hobbled to the fridge and paused, waiting for her to say something or stop me.

"Maybe when our children and your parents get here, it will help jog your memory."

*Great, that's all I need. More people to deal with.* I opened the fridge and looked inside. There was plenty of food and a variety of drinks. Everything was meticulously organized. "When are they coming over?" I asked as I snagged a cold can of Coke. Shutting the fridge, I popped the top and took a long swig.

"I called them from the nursing home, so they should be here any time."

As if on cue, I heard the front door open. Footsteps and muted voices approached.

She'd been watching me intently. "Do you really think you should be drinking Coke?"

In response, I lifted the can and took another long drink. "Ah, that's what I'm talking about," I said, wiping my mouth. I swallowed down a burp that tried sneaking out and set down the can.

She rolled her eyes and shook her head as four people walked into the dining room.

"Gregory," said a stern-looking, white-haired man. He stopped, folded his arms, and stared at me as if he was waiting for me to do or say something. His custom-made suit perfectly fit his slender body. The suit probably cost more than I'd spend for clothes in five years.

A trim woman, who looked a good twenty years younger than the man, held out her jeweled hands and hurried toward me. "Gregory, I'm so glad to see you're better." When she reached me, she took both my hands in hers and touched her cheek to mine. Backing up, she said, "Your father and I have been so worried about you."

"You're my mother?" I blurted.

Her eyes got big. "Of course, I'm your mother."

"I'm sorry," I said. "It's just that you look so . . . young."

"Thank you," she said with delight. "My last operation did wonders for me, didn't it?" Smiling, she showed me both sides of her face.

"You had a face lift?"

A young man, dressed almost exactly like me, stood behind them and laughed. "More like seven or eight of them."

The wispy, blonde-haired girl standing next to him slapped him on the arm. "Shut up." She turned to me. "I'm glad to see you're doing better." She looked to be in her mid-twenties and resembled Hilary in a lot of ways. She wore a multi-colored designer dress that hung to her knees and showed off her thin calves and expensive high heels.

"And you are?"

She gave me a blank stare.

Hilary sighed and placed her drink on the countertop. "It seems as though Gregory has a problem with his memory. He can't remember who he is or who we are."

"His memory had better return fast," said the man in the suit. "We have a meeting with the CEO of Standall Enterprises in two weeks. We're also having some problems with the new startup that we can't seem to resolve. Those people want to deal with you directly or, as they told us, 'No go.' "

Apparently, now that I was out of my coma, it was back to the grinding mill. No rest for the wicked, or the sickly. I took a sip of my drink, thinking I couldn't wait to get back to my simple lifestyle. How did I get linked up in this strange place anyway? I pinched myself again, but it hurt.

"A sugary drink, Gregory?" my supposed mother asked. "Are you trying to kill yourself?"

"What do you mean?"

"You know, you are not supposed to have soda pop or anything with sugar in it."

"Why? Do I have diabetes or something?"

"No, nothing that serious," Hilary replied.

The young girl giggled. "It makes you hyper as hell."

Dad glared at her.

*Aha. This is what I need to prove I'm not Greg.* I didn't get hyper when I drank Coke. Okay, maybe a little bit, but it wasn't bad enough to keep me from drinking one every now and then. It never interfered with my work. I didn't know if something like this would prove I wasn't Greg or not.

I didn't say anything at the moment though. I had an appointment with Eric and the doc in the morning. I would talk to Eric about it then. In the meantime, I walked to the sink and dumped the drink.

"Maybe he should go see Doctor Morrison." This from the young girl.

Hilary replied, "I've already made an appointment for Wednesday morning, Brittney, but I'm hoping his memory will return by then and we won't need to go."

Good. Now, I knew the girl's name: Brittney. "Who's Doctor Morrison?" I asked.

"He's the family psychiatrist," Brittney stated. "We've all been to see him."

"Really? A family psychiatrist? Doesn't that get kind of messy, with him knowing everybody's secrets?"

The old man blustered, "Doctor Morrison is a professional. He would never divulge anything that has been told to him in private. Besides, having someone who knows about the family dynamics is good. His knowledge of our family allows him to see the bigger picture." He focused a stern look on me. "You have responsibilities to the company and this family, Gregory. I expect you to be back in the office soon." He turned to his wife. "Are you ready to go?"

"Leaving so soon Mom and Dad?" I blurted. "You just got here." Secretly I was happy they were leaving. I was growing tired and wanted to lie down for a while.

Fire flared in the old man's eyes and his lips pressed into a fine line. "Watch your m—"

"I'm sorry, Gregory," Mom said, cutting the old man off. "We have other engagements." She patted his arm and gave him a nod of her head, as if saying, *Not now*. She turned to Hilary. "We'll talk later, okay? Bye everyone." The two of them turned and left without another word.

"We really should be going, too," Brittney said. "I have a Yoga class in an hour."

"Fine with me," the young man said.

"Okay, see you later, Brittney, and . . . I'm sorry, I didn't get your name," I said to the young man.

"Jonathan," he muttered with an amused smile as though I was an idiot. He walked off, followed by Brittney.

I went to the fridge and got another Coke.

Hilary raised her eyebrows.

"Don't say anything," I told her. "I'm not in the mood to be babied."

"Fine, fine." She held up a hand in defeat.

"So, who are Brittney and Jonathan? Am I related to them?"

Hilary seemed a little miffed. She took a deep breath. "I talked to you about them in the nursing home. They are two of our three children. Jonathan is the oldest, Brittney is the youngest. Our middle child, William, is at your office working."

"I take it he's the only one who works?"

"Don't start, Gregory."

I held up my hands in defense. "Sorry." After meeting my so-called family, I needed a touch of reality. "I'd like to make a phone call. Can I have some privacy?" Using my cane, I walked to the phone, sitting on the counter.

I swear, the temperature in the room dropped by ten

degrees when Hilary spoke. "Calling your girlfriend?"

"As a matter, of fact, I am. I'm also going to call my parents. My *real* parents."

"Gregory, why can't you remember—"

"Because I'm not Greg," I shot back. "I'm Brad. And in a few days, I'll prove it to you." I turned my back to her and picked up the phone. As I dialed, I heard her footsteps fading away down the hall. It was a relief she was gone.

Chrissy's phone rang three times. "Yo, what up?"

I hung up without saying a word. I had to get back to Arizona, fast.

# Chapter 17

## White Plains, NY

The weather was nice, so I took a nap in a chaise lounge by the pool and then spent an hour walking around the grounds with my cane. I knew it was crazy, but I wanted to see if anything looked familiar to me. Nope, nothing. I was Brad Jones and that was the end of it.

Hilary was sitting at the dining room table when I came inside for a drink of water. She had family photo albums stacked on one side of the table and was flipping through the one sitting in front of her.

*This is good,* I thought. My earliest memory was of my dad and me playing with a dog on our front lawn when I was about four years old. I had memories from that point up until the present moment. There was absolutely nothing she could show me that could erase those memories from my mind.

"I thought looking at some pictures might help jump-start your memory," she said, waving her hand toward an empty chair next to her.

"I guess it's worth a shot," I exclaimed, sitting down.

She partly closed the album so I could see the cover.

A sudden chill raced down my spine. The cover had a picture of what looked like me, Hilary, and two very young children, standing in front of this house. Hilary was holding a newborn baby in her arms. The title read: *April 23 1992: Brittney joins our family.*

April 23, 1992. That was Megan's birthday, too. My real daughter's birthday. Okay, this was kind of freaky. But seriously, I had to admit, other than the clothes, the guy in the picture looked identical to how I looked twenty-five years ago. Hilary looked younger, of course, and the house was a different color. How was all this possible?

Hilary opened the book. The man and woman claiming to be my parents were looking at the new baby. Mom was overly dramatic. In one picture, she actually had the back of her hand against her forehead as if she was swooning. Dad, he was stoic. Good to know he'd always been that way.

After that, I ignored every picture that didn't have me in it. It was really creepy seeing me in a life I had no recollection of living. How could this be? My memories were real. My parents in Golden were real. My daughter was real. I was real. But after an hour of flipping through photo albums covering Greg's whole life, from baby to fortyish husband and father, I was beginning to have doubts. How could I be so sure my name was Brad and that I lived a completely different life? Could I have dreamt Brad's life while in a coma? Was that even possible? A Google search might give me answers, but I wasn't comfortable asking Hilary if I could borrow a computer. I would ask Eric the next time I saw him.

"I didn't see any pictures of siblings. Do I have brothers or sisters?"

"No. You are an only child," Hilary said sharply as she closed the last album.

I nodded my head.

"None of these pictures—" She swept her hand over the albums. "—seemed familiar?"

I shrugged and shook my head.

She sighed. "Gregory, I don't—"

"What's with the *Gregory* thing?" I asked. "It's kind of weird. Why not Greg? It's more personal."

She rolled her eyes. "Your parents, well mine, too, don't believe in *nick-names* or shortened names. It's a family tradition. Haven't you noticed that everybody in the family has a name that could be shortened? But that no one ever uses the short version?"

"Not really," I replied as I tried to think of everybody's names: Brittany, Jonathan, who else?

"Think about it," she said. "My name's Hilary. You're Gregory. Your parents are Richard and Victoria."

"Richard?" I asked leaning forward in my seat.

"Yes, why?" she asked hopefully. "Does that ring a bell?"

"My dad, in Golden. His name is Richard, but everybody calls him Dick." I leaned back in my chair. I wasn't about to tell her my real mother's name was Vicky. She would read more into it than I cared to admit. She was also wrong about my name. My real name was Bradley, but ever since I could remember, I'd been called Brad. This had to be a coincidence, nothing more. "Go on," I said.

"Our children are Jonathan, William, and Brittney. I've never once heard anyone in our family shorten any of these names to Jon, Will, or Britt."

"Never?"

"No, never."

"Why? What would it hurt if I called Jonathan, Jon, or Brittney, Britt?"

"The way our parents see it, it's a class thing. Low-class people use nick-names. High-society people don't. And believe it or not, I don't agree with everything our parents say or do, but I have always respected how they wanted the names of their children and grandchildren expressed. So I've conceded and I prefer it that way.

Family dynamics can be . . . tricky."

She seemed to be getting uncomfortable, so I changed the subject. "Speaking of family, what about your mom and dad? Do you have brothers and sisters?"

She sat in silence for a moment, making me wonder if she'd heard me. Finally, she said without emotion, "When I was young, my parents traveled, a lot. Like you, I am an only child who was raised by nannies and maids. When I was old enough, I went to boarding school. My parents still travel, though not as much as they used to. We are not close. We talk on the phone occasionally, usually on my birthday and at Christmas time. I haven't seen them in two years."

She'd said it like she was reading from a book. She obviously resented how her parents had abandoned her when she was little. I didn't blame her. I would be bitter if my parents left me alone while they gallivanted around the world. It made me appreciate my parents, my real parents in Golden. There were always there for me, helping with school homework, attending school functions, seeing that I got to all my activities. I had an ideal childhood. Sure, there were disagreements, but every family had them. At least, we were together and remained close.

"I just had a thought," I said. "Did Greg ever go to Denver or Lake Havasu?"

Hilary thought for a moment. "He traveled a lot for business. Lake Havasu, I doubt. He could have gone to Denver though." Suddenly a little smile showed on her face. "Isn't that funny. I'm talking about Gregory like he is not you."

I chuckled with her. "The reason I asked, if I'm really Greg, but Greg has never been to Lake Havasu, how come I have all these memories of what Havasu looks like in my head?"

"Maybe Havasu doesn't look like what you are

picturing in your head. Maybe you are imagining what it looks like by using images you've seen on TV."

I shrugged. "Could be. But . . . the images in my mind are so real, so vivid, so detailed. I feel like I was there a few days ago, before I woke up in the nursing home. I'm not sure I could conjure up all the details for so many specific locations I can think of in Havasu."

"I don't know. Maybe when you were in the coma and your mind created Brad and his imagined life, it also created the setting for his life. It makes sense. Brad wouldn't be so real if he didn't have a place he thought of as home."

"I guess you're right," I said, not comforted by the thought my real life was all in my imagination. "I guess I'll know when I get to Havasu and compare my memories with the real town."

She frowned at the mention of me going to Havasu. "If you end up going, who knows, you may wake up tomorrow as Gregory. Memories and all."

"That's true."

She stood up. "It's almost dinner time. Are you hungry? I'll have Stella make us some dinner. What sounds good?" She pushed her chair under the table.

I shrugged. "I don't know what you have here, so I don't know what my choices are. Who's Stella?"

"Our live-in cook and maid."

"She lives here? In the house?"

"No, of course not," she retorted impatiently. "When you were walking outside, did you see the house in the backyard?"

There had been a house. It sat in the far back corner of the property. "I assumed it was a guest house."

"Stella and her family live there. Her husband, Nick, is our grounds keeper and maintenance man. It's convenient having them close by."

"Her family? Do they have kids?" I don't know why I

asked. Maybe it was because I hadn't seen any signs of kids in the yard. Like bikes, wagons, bats, and balls, you know, the kinds of things kids leave lying around yards when they are done with them.

Hilary looked thoughtful. "I don't know," she finally said. "I've never thought to ask." She picked up the phone and punched in three numbers. After waiting for a few seconds, she said, "We're ready for dinner now." And she hung up the phone.

"That was kind of rude wasn't it?" I asked.

"What?"

"I assume that was Stella you called?"

"Yes."

"You were kind of blunt with her, weren't you?"

"What do you mean?"

"No 'Hi, Stella. We're ready for dinner whenever you can get over here and get it made. Okay, thank you, bye,' or anything nice."

"Oh, I see your problem." She crossed her arms. "If you are *nice* to the help they will take advantage of you. If you treat them like employees, they will act like employees."

I could tell she firmly believed this and I wasn't about to argue with her. No wonder Hilary didn't know if Stella had kids or not.

Stella turned out to be a large-boned, austere-looking woman in her mid-thirties who spoke as little as possible. She wore plain clothes consisting of a dark gray skirt, a white button-up blouse, and black loafer-type shoes. Her dark hair had been pulled back into a ponytail. She wore very little, if any, makeup. She didn't fit my image of a maid. The scars on her hands and the deep creases in her drawn face made her look like she'd had a hard life. Maybe she used to live a wild life with parties, drinking, and drugs.

While she was out of the room, I asked Hilary about

her.

"She hasn't been here very long. Two years I think," Hilary said. "Our old maid suddenly took ill and we had to replace her on short notice. It just so happened that Stella and Nick were recommended by another couple we know. They told us Stella and Nick were trying to get out of their old life. Seems they were involved with a gang in Chicago and had had enough. I didn't want to hire them, but you insisted. You wanted to give them a chance to have a new life. You said they could start right away, and if they didn't work out, we could always replace them."

"I've heard it's hard to break away from gangs. Were there any repercussions?"

"No, not that I know of. But then again, unless one of them said something to me, how would I know? I think they still have contact with some of their old gang members because, every now and then, we would see one of them coming or going to the house out back. I was skeptical about the whole situation at first, but everything turned out fine as far as I can tell."

"No drive-by shootings or hoodie-wearing thugs hanging around the neighborhood, huh?" I teased.

She scowled. "Not hardly. And, by the way, Nick has been neglecting the tasks I ask him to do around the house. It's like he totally ignores my requests. I'm glad you are back so you can straighten him out."

Stella came back into the room, forcing us to move on to other topics of conversation.

\* \* \*

After dinner, I hobbled behind Hilary as she took me upstairs. "This is our bedroom," she said as we walked into a huge room with striking woven rugs thrown over the polished wooden floor.

A king-sized bed with nightstands on each side dominated the far wall. An L-shaped makeup table with a pink ruffled cover nestled neatly into one corner. Two doors, which I assumed were walk-in closets, and a long dresser took up the wall to my left. To my right, I could see a palatial bathroom through an arched doorway.

I spun around. Another long dresser sat near the entry door. Finely woven doilies, knick-knacks, and lamps covered the tops of the dressers. A couple of pictures and mirrors hung on the walls. It was a room of expensive furniture and elegant décor.

Suddenly, I had a terrible thought. *Does she expect me to sleep with her? In the same bed?* I hoped not.

"When you're ready, you can shower and shave," she said as she walked into the bathroom. "If you can't find what you need, ask me and I'll show you where it's at."

An unusually beautiful geometric mosaic with golden inlays had been designed into the beige-colored tile in the middle of the bathroom floor. I stopped and admired it. Then, I said to Hilary, "Do I stink? Do I need a shower?"

"No, I didn't mean that. It's just that . . . well, you always showered and shaved before dinner, but since the routine was upset today by your returning home, I thought you might like to do it now."

"Greg might have, but I don't. Construction can be dirty. I usually shower immediately after I get home from work to get the sawdust, the dirt, and the grime off my hair and skin. Sometimes, it's a few hours before I eat dinner."

"Right, the other life thing." She leaned against the marble counter and crossed her arms.

The unresolved sleeping arrangements worried me. "I . . . um . . . well." I cleared my throat. "Sleeping in the same bed with you is going to be a little uncomfortable for me. Do you have a spare bedroom I could stay in for a while?"

She looked at the bed, certainly big enough for both of us to have our own space, then she looked at me. She sighed in frustration and shook her head in disappointment. Obviously, she was anxious to get her husband back.

I didn't blame her. If I was in her position I would be anxious, too. I didn't want to alienate her, but I really didn't want to sleep next to her either. She was a woman and a stranger.

I also had to face the facts. At the moment, I needed her help. I had nothing. Not even decent clothes. If I walked out the door and left right now, I had no money and no way to get anywhere, except by foot alone. Couldn't get to Havasu that way. Come to think of it, I didn't even have I.D. No drivers license, no social security card, no credit card, nothing.

Hilary uncrossed her arms and took a step forward. "I suppose you could sleep in one of the spare bedrooms for a night or two." She was obviously disappointed.

"Great. Thanks."

"But I've got to tell you, Gregory." She held up a hand, warding off my objection to being called Greg. "I've been waiting for you to come out of your coma for weeks. I am willing to wait a few more days. But, as you know, I am not a patient woman. I want my life back. Do you understand?"

"Let's see what the next few days brings, okay? Now, why don't you show me where my room is?"

She spun around and walked out of the bathroom, through the bedroom door, and down the hall. She stepped into another bedroom. Sweeping her arm to indicate the room, she said, "Will this do?"

It looked like another master bedroom, this one a little less dramatic in color and décor. A queen-sized bed was centered on one wall, flanked by oak nightstands on each side. A lush beige carpet covered the floor. A mirrored dresser, cushioned set of chairs and flat-screen TV rounded out the furniture. To the left, there was an arched bathroom doorway and a closet. While not quite as fancy as Hilary's room, it was more than fancy enough for me. I would have been comfortable sleeping on a cot in the garage if it meant not having to sleep with Hilary.

"By the way, the faucet in this bathroom is dripping. Nick supposedly bought a new one but he hasn't gotten around to installing it yet. One of those tasks that he's been putting off. I hope the dripping doesn't bother you."

"I'm sure it won't."

"Good. See you in the morning." She turned and left, shutting the door and leaving me to fend for myself.

*I have to get out of here and back to Arizona. Fast.*

# Chapter 18

White Plains, NY

Sometime in the middle of the night, I jerked up out of a troubled sleep, drenched in a cold sweat. The nightmare about Hilary, dressed in a skimpy nightie, coming into my room and climbing into bed with me, scared me more than almost any other nightmare I could have had. Needless to say, I tossed and turned the rest of the night.

But to be fair, my restless night couldn't be completely blamed on the nightmare. The dripping faucet bothered me more than I'd expected. I was also worried about Chrissy, my parents, my daughter, and Sadie. They had to be going crazy wondering what happened to me and wondering if I was okay or not. It agonized me that I couldn't get in touch with them.

Again, I resolved to get to Arizona as soon as possible.

When morning came, I snuck downstairs with my cane and grabbed a hot cup of coffee, which I assumed Stella had made. I returned to my room, shaved, and hopped in the shower. Luckily for me, my bedroom had its own bathroom, so I didn't have to share Hilary's. I needed a change of clothes. I checked the adjacent closet. Empty, except for extra blankets and pillows. No clothing of any kind.

I dressed in the Dockers and shirt she had given me

yesterday, but I didn't want to wear them around all day. I wasn't sure if I should go into Hilary's bedroom and explore the walk-in closets for clean clothes. If I didn't check out her closets, though, I'd be stuck in this annoying attire. I had to take a chance.

I looked down the hall and her bedroom door was open. I peaked inside and didn't see Hilary anywhere. The water wasn't running in the bathroom, so she wasn't taking a shower. I knocked and called out her name quietly, just to make sure she wasn't there and wouldn't hear me from downstairs either. With no response, I walked across the room to the first walk-in closet and opened the door. Nope, this was packed full of Hilary's clothes: tops, suits, dresses, and gowns. Rows of high-end fashion shoes lined two long shelves. *How could anyone ever wear this many clothes and shoes?*

I opened the other closet door and flipped on the light. All of the clothes hanging on hangers were businessmen clothes: Dockers, suits, white button-up shirts, and polo shirts. Right away, I knew I wouldn't be comfortable wearing any of these.

Built-in drawers sat in one corner. I opened each drawer, one at a time, looking for something that would be comfortable, like blue jeans and a colored T-shirt. No luck. The only T-shirts Greg owned were white. And as far as I could tell, he didn't own one pair of blue jeans. *What kind of man doesn't own blue jeans?*

I found the same problem with shoes, dress-type shoes. No sneakers. No cowboy boots. I didn't see any sweat pants or running shoes either. But maybe he kept them in a different location, separate from his everyday clothes.

It looked like the first thing on my list of things to do today was to go shopping. I wasn't about to keep wearing Greg's dressy clothes. They were far from my style and I didn't feel comfortable in them. And if truth be known, I wanted my new clothes to make the statement that I *wasn't* Greg. I was Brad.

Another part of my mind modified this thought. *It might make things easier if I pretend to be Greg. It will give me access to money, cars, and anything else I might need to get to Arizona. The flip side of this is that if I pretend to be Greg, Hilary will want me to sleep with her. I am going to have to walk a fine line of deception where she is concerned.*

Pretending to be Greg was a smart idea, I decided. As long as I played my cards right, I figured it would be the easiest way to get what I wanted. Decision made, I turned off the light and closed the door without changing clothes.

*　*　*

My legs were getting stronger, so I walked down the stairs without my cane this time. A few days of working out and I could probably get them in shape faster.

When I walked into the kitchen, Stella was cooking breakfast at the stove. The smell of bacon and toast filled the air.

At the table, Hilary sat reading the newspaper.

"Good morning," I said cheerfully as I walked to the coffeemaker.

Stella nodded at me in recognition of my presence but didn't say anything.

"Good morning, *Gregory*. How did you sleep?" Hilary's tone of voice was anything but pleasant. In fact, it bordered on rude.

I couldn't help but notice the emphasis she put on Gregory. It made me want to cringe. If she insisted on calling me Gregory, I would let her. I wasn't going to be in this house very long anyway.

"I tossed and turned quite a bit," I said. "I think it was because I wasn't used to the bed. The dripping faucet didn't help."

"Yes, probably so." A faint frown appeared at the corners of her lips as she looked me over with dismay. "You're wearing the same clothes you wore yesterday. You have clean clothes in your closet."

"Yes, I know. By the way," I said as I poured coffee in a cup that was sitting on the counter, "I assume I have a wallet with a drivers license and stuff in it?"

"Of course. It's in a tray on top of your dresser in *our* bedroom," she said coldly.

I ignored the jab. I had other things on my mind, like why she wasn't surprised I wanted the wallet. But then again, in her mind, I was Greg and the wallet was mine. I had every right to it. I felt a little guilty at the thought of using Greg's wallet, but at this point, I had to do what I had to do, no matter how I felt about it. "Okay, good. I was thinking of going out this morning. Maybe do some shopping."

She sat back and stared at me in shock. "You? Shopping? You hate shopping. You always send me or Stella when you need something."

Stella remained stoic at the kitchen sink and wisely stayed out of the conversation. No doubt, she'd learned a long time ago to keep her mouth shut when Hilary was around.

"Well, uh . . . I thought that getting out and seeing some of the town might refresh my memories. I thought I would also drive past Greg's . . . my office building and see if it brings back memories. Then I want to stop at a store and pick up a few things."

"Like what?"

"Clothes. You know, jeans, T-shirts, shoes."

Astounded, she sat up straighter. "You have a closet full of clothes upstairs. Why would you need more?"

"I know, I just looked at them. But I didn't see anything I want to wear, like blue jeans, a colored T-shirt, and some comfortable shoes."

Clearly irritated, Hilary nagged at me, "You hate colored T-shirts and jeans. You are the one who always said that the easiest way to tell if someone is low class, just look at what they wear: colored T-shirts and jeans."

Now I was getting mad that Hilary was going to resist everything I wanted to do. How would Greg handle this situation, I wondered. Would he cower and back down? For some reason, I didn't think so. He was a successful businessman who was used to the pressure of multimillion-dollar deals. I doubted if he would let Hilary dominate him on everything, including the clothes he wore.

Thinking back to yesterday, when Hilary chided me for drinking a sugary drink, I wondered if Greg let her dominate little things, like what he ate and drank. Possibly. But I didn't think he would let her tell him what to wear, what he did with his time, or where he went.

"I'm glad you are going to drive past the company building, but I don't get this attitude of yours about the clothes."

The tone of her voice and her body posture told me she was in an argumentative mood. I didn't want to fight, so I decided to take a different approach to see what would happen. Glaring at her, I stated in a low, firm voice, "I want different clothes to wear. So I'm going shopping this morning and that's final."

Her brows raised. Her mouth dropped open. She seemed to shrink in on herself. "Okay," she replied meekly.

I hid my shock that she gave in so quickly. Maybe putting my foot down and telling her exactly what I was going to do was the answer to controlling her. I'd have to try it again to be sure though.

Stella chose that moment to serve breakfast. Eggs, toast, hash browns, and orange juice seemed sufficient for some people, but not enough for me. I liked a working man's meal with bacon, ham, or steak. This meager breakfast would tide me over until I got out of the house. Then I'd stop and get a donut or sweet roll.

As I finished eating, I stood up, anxious to get going. Then I realized I didn't know where I was going or how I was getting there. "Um, is there a shopping center close by? Close enough to walk to?"

"That depends on what kind of store you are looking for," Hilary said, wiping some egg yolk up with the last of her toast.

"A Wal-Mart or a K-Mart would do."

Hilary rolled her eyes. "We don't shop at those stores."

I stared at her in silence, waiting for an answer.

She sighed. "There's a discount store like that about two miles from here. I'm not sure which one it is." She pushed away from the table and stood up, preparing to leave.

"Do you have a car I could borrow . . . or something?"

She took a deep breath and let it out slowly. "Your car is in the garage."

"Which is . . . where?" I asked, looking for a door that might lead to the garage.

"Oh, hell. Follow me." She brushed past me and walked down the hall. She opened a door and walked through.

I followed more slowly on my weakened legs until I found myself in a pure white sterile garage. *Sterile* because the only things in it to be seen were two cars: a Cadillac Escalade and a Mercedes S-Class Coupe, both pure black. I stood there like an idiot, looking around at the emptiness.

"Is something wrong?" Hilary asked.

"No. It's just that . . . well . . . this garage has got to be the cleanest, least-cluttered garage I've ever seen."

"Of course it is. Rich people don't have *clutter*."

"When I was growing up, our garage had shelving on all the walls and they were piled high with boxes containing everything from camping equipment to Christmas decorations. There were work benches along one of the walls for all the tools. We even had stuff hanging from the ceiling. I've never seen a garage that wasn't used for storage."

The whole time I was talking Hilary, looked at me like I was crazy. "I don't know what you're talking about. Is this something *Brad* made up?"

I ignored her jab at my name. "Don't you at least store things like hand tools, the lawn mower, and rakes and stuff in here?"

"Those are kept in the gardener's shed, where they belong," she muttered.

"Of course, they are. How stupid of me to think otherwise."

Instead of acknowledging my sarcastic comment, she pointed to the Mercedes. "That one is yours. The keys are in it." She turned abruptly to go back into the house.

"Wait, does it have a GPS in it?"

"Of course, it does."

"Does the GPS have the office building and home programmed into it?"

She sighed in frustration. "I don't know. I'll give you the addresses, just in case."

"Okay, great. I'd hate to get lost and not be able to find the office or get back here."

She went inside without saying anything more.

I waited a few moments, then went into the house and looked in the kitchen and dining rooms. Hilary was nowhere to be seen. I hurried up the stairs, hoping Hilary wasn't in her bedroom. I lucked out.

Glancing around the room, I saw a wallet sitting on one of the dressers. I picked it up, opened it, and saw it contained plenty of cash, at least five or six hundred dollars, probably more. There was also a drivers license, three or four credit cards, a debit card, and numerous other cards. At this point, I was only interested in the cash. In fact, I thought about leaving all the cards on the dresser. I wouldn't feel comfortable using Greg's debit card. I didn't know his pin number or any other information I might get asked if I used one. Plus, what if I had to sign his name?

In the end, I left the cards in the wallet and headed back downstairs. On the kitchen counter, I found a piece of paper with addresses for the office and home. Better still, I saw no sign of Hilary as I scooted for the garage.

I opened the Mercedes door and slid into the seat. The leather seats smelled wonderful. The keys were sitting on the center console, next to the gear shifter. I picked them up and started the car. I opened the garage door with the remote on the visor and backed the car out into the driveway.

I let the engine idle while I messed with the GPS. It was actually pretty simple to operate and, in no time, I had it programmed to go to the nearest Wal-Mart. I also made sure that it had *home* programmed into it before I left. I didn't bother programming in the office. I'd only told Hilary I was going to drive by to make her feel better about me going out.

It felt strange driving a vehicle other than my truck. Don't get me wrong. The car was smooth and silent and rode like a dream. But I liked my truck better. It was more my style.

The trip to the store and back was non-eventful. In under one hour, I picked up some jeans, T-shirts, and shoes and was back at the house with my new clothes.

# Chapter 19

White Plains, NY

When I walked into Doctor Morrison's office, it didn't surprise me that the office looked like the stereotypical psychiatrist's office I'd seen in movies. Dark wood paneling covered the walls. Heavy burgundy drapes blocked the sunlight, leaving the room dim and cozy.

It wasn't my idea to come talk to him. Hilary and Greg's parents told me, in no uncertain terms, that I was going to this appointment, If I didn't, they would get their attorneys involved, something about being declared mentally unstable and unable to make decisions on my own. I didn't want that. I wanted to go back to Arizona as soon as possible. This appointment was just to satisfy them so I could move forward on my plans.

It had been three days since I'd left Whispering Pines. Each day, I did the exercises recommended by the physical therapist and worked out in the basement exercise room at Hilary's house. I could feel myself growing stronger. I no longer used my cane. And best of all, I now wore jeans, a T-shirt, and comfortable shoes.

When the session started, the doctor sat with his legs crossed in a brown leather-covered chair facing a matching couch. He had me lie down on the couch.

Staring at the ceiling fan slowly rotating, I told him my story. About halfway through, I almost quit because he hadn't made a sound. I wondered if he was really listening to me, if he was thinking about something or someone else. He sat facing me in his chair with his eyes down. Not knowing if I should interrupt his thoughts, I looked back at the fan and kept going.

"So . . ." he said when I stopped talking. He uncrossed his legs and looked me in the eye. "You really believe you are this Brad Jones?"

"Like I told you, I have all the memories of Brad and none of Greg. How could I believe anything else?"

He made a note on a pad of paper sitting on his lap.

I didn't tell him about my real parents' names being nicknames for Greg's parents. No sense in giving him information he may be able to use against my argument.

"Let's say, hypothetically, that you are Gregory."

"Okay."

"Did you like your life?"

"No."

"Why not?"

I glanced sideways at him. "You've met my family, right?"

He ignored my sarcasm. "You know I have. They are wonderful people."

I raised my eyebrows.

"Of course," he added, "they all have their little . . . shall we say, flaws."

I rolled my eyes. "You can say that again."

He cleared his throat. "Let's get back to you. Hilary said she showed you the family photo albums."

I waited for him to continue. I'm sure he wanted me to come clean and admit that I was Greg, but I couldn't do that.

Finally, he said, "So . . . after seeing the photographs of you from childhood onward, how can you claim to be Brad?"

"Easy. I have all the memories from Brad's life and none from Greg's. Brad's life feels right. Greg's life feels wrong."

"Hmmm. I'm wondering if hypnosis will jog your memories, restore your mind to its former self."

Suddenly, I saw where this was going to end up. It had all been arranged. They weren't going to quit until they had Greg back. Therapy, hypnosis, drugs. How far would they go? I had the feeling that if I kept claiming so adamantly to be Brad, they would declare me mentally unstable anyway. I couldn't have that. Whatever it took to get back to Arizona, I would have to do. Just like I had started doing with Hilary, I was going to have to pretend to be Greg to the doctor.

Doctor Morrison had been talking about a bunch of different procedures available to him, but I hadn't been paying attention.

I interrupted him. "You're right."

"Excuse me? I'm right about what?"

"Me being Greg. I just realized that I have to be Greg."

"Yes, go on."

"I mean, how could so many people know me as Greg if I'm not really him? And what about all the photos? Kind of hard to ignore them." I hesitated about saying my next thoughts, but I blurted them out anyway to be more convincing. "There's also the fact that I can't get a hold of my parents, or Brad's parents or anyone that Brad knew. It's almost like . . . they don't exist."

He'd been staring hard at me since I'd started talking. He slowly nodded his head. "Faced with hypnosis or drugs, which would obviously prove who you really are, you are realizing that there's no way you can keep this charade up. So I'm asking you again, are you Gregory? Or are you Brad?"

Not good. He wanted a firm commitment that, in all honesty, I couldn't make. I had to fudge a little. "I'm . . . confused." Unable to lie still for another minute under his stare, I got up off the couch and paced across the floor. "I admit, I still think of myself as Brad. But deep down, I must be Greg. Give me a little time, but I think eventually I will be able to think of myself as Greg."

His eyes perked up and he seemed to come alive for the first time. I almost laughed at the priceless look on his face. His mind seemed to read: *Breakthrough in one session!* A feather in his cap with the family.

*Great. If that's what he wants to think, let him. If it makes him happy and he lets me go with no restrictions, that's what I want.*

At that point, our time was up. He ushered me to the door and said, "We made good progress today, Gregory. Make an appointment with my secretary for next week at this same time, and we'll see if we can continue our progress."

I thanked him and made the appointment with the secretary. By next week at this time, I was going to be in Arizona, far, far away from these nutty people and their crazy world.

\* \* \*

Later that afternoon, I sat at the kitchen table thinking about the differences between me and Greg. I hadn't considered it before, but if I was really Greg, who it appeared had never done a day of physical labor in his life, how come I knew so much about construction? In my life, I was a licensed general contractor. Instead of building new homes, I specialized in the independent handyman jobs.

I liked the challenge of taking on a problem and fixing it. True, tearing out old carpet and installing tile wasn't a real problem, but there were always little issues, problems, if you will, that popped up on every job. I liked the low overhead, I didn't have to arrange for construction loans or deal with sub-contractors. The only person I had to deal with were the homeowners, and I usually enjoyed talking with them.

So, if I was really Greg, how could I know how to do all the things I could do? I looked around. I knew how to replace everything I could see, from the chandelier hanging over the dining room table to the kitchen sink, not that they needed to be replaced in a well-maintained upscale house like this. But just to reassure myself I really knew my business, I reviewed in my mind how to replace the hanging light and the sink. Without a doubt, I knew how to take the old ones out and install new ones. One more strike against Greg. I had to be Brad.

Hilary walked into the room. She winced at my casual attire. "Happy with your shopping spree yesterday?" she sneered, sitting down across the table from me.

I wasn't going there, no way, no how. Instead, I replied, "I was thinking about everything Doctor Morrison and I had talked about today. I've got to admit, I think I'm more confused now than I was yesterday."

A glimmer of hope registered in her brown eyes. "Oh, Gregory, I know it's hard for you to remember our life." She leaned forward and clasp her hands on the table in front of her as if she was trying to control herself. "But you need to try. I realize you're having a hard time adjusting to everything. But I am, too. I don't care what you have to do, you need to get beyond this. I want our life back the way it was before you were in a coma."

I had been dreading what I was about to say, but after her little rant, I felt like it didn't matter much what I did. I had started my scheme by telling Doctor Morrison that I thought I must be Greg. Now, I was going to continue to enhance the lie with Hilary. As much as I didn't like her, I didn't hate her exactly, but I didn't like myself for lying to her. I knew if I kept insisting on being Brad, I might never get back to Arizona.

"Doctor Morrison helped me a lot today," I said slowly. "In fact, I had kind of a breakthrough."

She shifted in her seat. I could tell she was chomping at the bit to ask me what had happened, but she kept her emotions in check, waiting for me to explain.

"I realized I have to be Greg."

She came halfway to her feet. Little "Oh's" of excitement escaped from her lips.

I held up my hands, motioning for her to sit back down. "I know this must be wonderful news to you, and I don't blame you for being excited, but I still don't have any of Greg's memories. Maybe in time I will, but for now, I can't remember anything about his life."

She had warmed up . . . a little bit. "When you were lying in the nursing home, I would sit with you and talk about our life, our children, our problems. Eric said you couldn't hear me, but I believed you could. When I rubbed your hand, ran my fingers through your hair, or gave you a sponge bath, you reacted by moving or pulling away . . . "

Chills raced down my spine. My heart pounded in my chest. My blood ran cold at her words.

" . . . and I knew you were reacting to me and what I was doing. Eric wouldn't believe me. He had the doctor run some tests to prove it. The old coot ran a pen up and down your foot. He poked your foot with a pen. You didn't respond to anything he did. After he left, I did the pen test myself. And you responded! You responded only to what I did."

*That's what you think, lady,* I screamed in my mind. I was so stunned by what she was saying and the memories that were flooding into my mind, I couldn't speak.

"You needed that contact with someone you knew,"

she said. "I knew it would help, and I was right."

"Well . . . ," I stumbled, trying to gather myself together. "This is an interesting development."

"What do you mean?"

"Before I was in the coma, I started having these *funny feelings* on different parts of my body."

Her eyes got wide. "Don't tell me? You could feel what I was doing?"

"I think so."

She clasped her fists and lifted them in the air in a sign of triumph. "I knew it was a good thing to do."

"I'm not sure it was a good thing or not," I replied. "The way I see it, if I could feel you touching Greg's body, how could I, Brad, experience those feelings out in Arizona?"

"This just proves that you're not Brad. You're Gregory," she barked with hostility. "There's no other rational explanation."

The dining room was growing dark as the sun was setting, but neither one of us made a move to turn on a light. We sat in heated silence, the air thick and explosive between us.

It was getting hard to see her face and I was glad she couldn't see mine. I was sure my feelings were showing, and they weren't happy ones. I felt like every person and animal I'd ever known and loved had died, all at the same time. And in a way, they had. I couldn't come up with a logical explanation to convince myself that, as Brad, I could feel what was happening to Greg's body from thousands of miles away.

It took me a moment to realize that Hilary was speaking again.

"Before the wreck that put—"

"Wreck?" I interrupted, sitting upright on my chair.

"Yes. The wreck that put you in your coma."

A wave of déjà vu passed through me. Suddenly, I

remembered something. I stood up and walked to the counter. "I was in a wreck . . . in Arizona. Yes . . . I remember now." I whirled around to face her. "Before waking up in the nursing home room, I was driving down the road. A car veered across the yellow line into my lane. It happened so fast, there was nothing I could do to prevent it."

Even in the dim light, I saw her eyes get big. "That's exactly what happened to Gregory! I mean . . . you or . . . "

I smiled. "That's okay. I know what you're trying to say." As I walked back toward my chair, everything about my accident came back to me, clear as a bell. But something, didn't seem right. I put both hands on the back of the chair and leaned forward. "What date was it when Greg got in the wreck?"

She thought for a second. "It was August twenty-seventh. I remember because it was two days after I came back from a trip to Hawaii."

"This is strange," I replied. Sitting down, I rested my forearms on the table. "You claim Greg was in a coma for three weeks, but I was in my wreck on September eighteenth. And yet, I woke up the next day."

"That is strange," she said. "How did you come up with that date?"

"I'd just left a doctor's office. I'd gone to see him about my funny feelings. I decided to take a drive out to the freeway and think about things."

"I don't know what to say about that," she replied, shifting restlessly in her seat, perhaps because of her discomfort with this topic of conversation. "The accident was on August twenty-seventh."

I didn't know what to think about it either. Not that it was a big deal. But the inconsistency in time bothered me. Maybe it was something that would clear itself up eventually. Leaning back in my chair, I asked, "Was

Greg by himself when he had the wreck?"

"Yes. Why?"

"He was driving his own car?"

"Yes." She looked confused.

"What about the Mercedes? It's sitting out in the garage in perfectly good shape."

She laughed, relief flooding her face. No doubt, she'd been uncomfortable talking about the time inconsistency. "We get new cars every year. It was time to upgrade anyway, so after the insurance company paid the claim, I had a brand-new black Mercedes brought over from the dealership. It looks just like the one that was wrecked."

I was still baffled by the relationship between Greg's accident and mine. I wasn't sure what more to ask or say about it.

"Oh, by the way," Hilary said, "speaking of new and upgrading. Nick came to me and said the faucet fixtures he'd bought for the guest bathroom were missing from the shed. He went up to check the leaky faucet, but it was no longer dripping. And the faucet had been replaced with the fixtures he'd bought. Do you know anything about that?"

"Sure." I shrugged. "I was bored after I got back from Morrison's office. I got the tools and the faucet fixtures from the shed and replaced it. I hope that's okay."

She rolled her eyes. "Gregory, you know how we, your parents and I, feel about doing manual labor. That's for the hired help. That's why we pay them."

"Greg might have felt that way, but I don't. Why is replacing a leaky faucet such a big deal?"

She sighed. "Years ago, before we met, while you were in college, you worked as a *laborer* for a handyman."

My ears perked up. "And that was a bad thing?"

"Yes, it was. You know that blue-collar labor for people of our standing is . . . frowned upon."

My eyes narrowed on her. "Yes, I'm sure it is."

"To make matters worse, you lied to your parents. You told them you were working as an apprentice in a large corporation. For three full years, you were into all kinds of filthy things: plumbing, lighting, and flooring. When we started dating, you lied to me, too. You didn't think I noticed the cuts and blisters on your rough dry hands. Those didn't come from working in an office. We were seeing each other almost every night, so it wasn't something you could hide from me. With my insistence, you finally confessed."

"And did Greg stop?"

"Yes . . . after I told you in no uncertain terms that, if you kept working as a laborer, I was leaving, I didn't want to be hanging around with *hired help* or marry someone associated with a low-class job. I believe, if it hadn't been for me telling you that you had to quit, you'd still be doing it today. I saved you from a life of drudgery."

The news about Gregory working for a handyman wasn't good. It explained how I could have learned everything I needed to know to be a handyman. Greg had experience with all the things I loved to do. I looked at Hilary. "If it bothers you that much, I won't fix anything else around the house. But I've got to find something to do or I'll go nuts. I'm not the type to sit around and do nothing all day. Any suggestions?"

"Work on giving me back my life," she demanded as she stood up.

The clicking of her heels in the hallway slowly faded away as I sat in the dark alone. So many feelings washed over me. How did the car wreck play into all this? Was Brad's life dead, just like Greg's life seemed to be dead? I didn't know how much more of this I could take.

# Chapter 20

## White Plains, NY

A week had passed since I'd left the nursing home. I was feeling much better. My muscle mass was returning due to working out daily in the exercise room in the basement of the house. Despite Hilary's daily protests, I was still sleeping in the guest room. I had managed to avoid the rest of the family by being conveniently busy or gone when they stopped by. I wondered if Hilary was glad about that, being that I wore clothes not approved of by the family.

After talking with Hilary about the accident, I'd had a rough few days and nights. It took a long time for me to come to terms with the fact that I had felt Hilary touching and rubbing Greg's hands and body. I still couldn't explain it. Even after giving it a lot of thought, I decided that I still had to be Brad. My memories were too strong, too emotional, and too thorough to be anything but real. I still believed I had two living parents, a daughter, a dog, and a girlfriend who loved me. I wasn't ready to give up on my life as Brad yet.

Throughout the week, I had tried calling Chrissy and my family, but like before, no results. I was really getting concerned. I hated to think of them wondering where I was and if I was okay, but there was nothing I could do about it until I could get out of here and go there in person.

Hilary continued to call me Gregory, which bothered me, but I couldn't force the issue if I was going to play the role of Greg. Even though I didn't have any of Greg's memories, I was one-hundred-percent Greg in her mind.

If I went back to insisting I was Brad, the family would call in the psychiatrists and lawyers and possibly confine me, not allow me to leave on my own. But if they continued to believe that I thought I must be Greg, they wouldn't have any reason to keep me from leaving.

To leave town, I would have to travel as Greg Nordmeyer because I didn't have any ID for Brad. My biggest concern was telling Hilary that I wanted to go to the Denver area and then on to Arizona. I feared how she might react. As luck would have it, she brought it up that night while we were eating dinner.

As Stella cleared away the empty dinner plates and prepared the dessert, Hilary said, "I was wondering what you could do that might help clear up this confusion you have about this life you think you had as Brad."

A little nervous about where she might go with this, I remained quiet.

"You claim to have parents and a daughter in Denver?"

"Yeah," I replied hesitantly, weary of a trap."They live in Golden, a suburb of Denver."

"Why don't you go there to see if you can find them? After all, you haven't been able to get them on the phone. Go to the house you claim you were raised in, where you claim they still live. Prove to yourself, once and for all, that they are just a figment of your imagination, brought on by hallucinations while you were in the coma. Then you can come back home, and we can get on with our lives."

I almost jumped up and shouted for joy. This was perfect. I'd been so worried about how she was going to react when I expressed that I wanted to go and try to find my family. And here she was, offering me the opportunity to go.

*Hmmm. How convenient. Too convenient?* Living in the same house with her for the last week, I'd gotten to know her well enough to know that this probably wasn't her idea, but I didn't want to counter her offer with anything negative. Better to act nonchalant about it. For some reason, I had a feeling the suggestion had come from Doctor Morrison.

I pondered the idea for a moment, as if I was giving it some thought. "That sounds like it might work." I had to bite my tongue to keep the smile off my face.

Stella set a piece of German chocolate cake on the table in front of me. It looked so delicious, it helped distract my attention.

"Of course," Hilary said in a commanding tone, "I would expect you to come straight home from Denver as soon as possible."

*Ah ha! There it is. She is fine with me going to Denver to try to find my parents and daughter, but she doesn't want me going to Arizona to try to find Chrissy.* Could it be that deep down she was a little worried I really was Brad, and that if I would find Chrissy, I'd stay in Arizona? Could be. Better to play along and not rock the boat.

"Of course," I said. "A quick trip, there and back. Two or three days is all I should need." I could care less about how many days she planned for me to be gone. As soon as I was in Denver, I would be with family. That's all I cared about.

A doubtful look crossed her face. "I would think one day should suffice. Usually, we have an agent at the company who handles all the travel, but in this case, I will arrange your travel itinerary myself. When would you like to leave?"

I was so excited, I could hardly think. "Would tomorrow be too soon?" I took a big bite of cake.

"It depends. I suppose the sooner you go, the better. I will check and let you know after dinner. In the meantime, why don't you go up and pack your clothes? I'm sure I can get you a flight out, if not tomorrow, the next day."

"Sounds good to me." I finished my cake and when out of her sight, I danced up to my room. This was wonderful. I feared I was going to have to fight with her in order to leave by myself, but her offering it to me made my day.

\* \* \*

As soon as I walked into my room, I saw an overnight bag sitting on the bed. Either Hilary or Stella had put it there. I chuckled to myself. Hilary had known all the while I would go. Of course, it was pretty obvious that I wanted to go, given how much I worried about Mom, Dad, Megan, and Chrissy. Oh, and Sadie, too.

I picked up the bag. As far as I was concerned, the only clothes I needed were the clothes on my back and the T-shirts and extra pair of jeans I'd bought the other day. Once I got to my parents' place in Golden. and let them know I was okay, I could go on to Arizona. At my house, I would find everything I needed.

I shoved my new clothes into the bag, along with my toothbrush, tooth paste, a razor, shaving cream, and deodorant. I needed nothing else. After all, I was finally heading home.

I sat on the bed and turned on the TV just to have some noise in the room. It helped me pass the time.

Finally, there was a knock at the door and Hilary opened it. She stopped just inside the doorway and looked down at a paper she held in her hand. "Your flight leaves the day after tomorrow in the morning at seven. It's a four-hour, non-stop flight to Denver. With the time zone change, you'll arrive at nine-fifteen."

"Okay, good deal."

"I reserved a room for two nights for you at the Brown Palace Hotel." She spoke in a stiff and formal tone, like she was a secretary giving me my itinerary for a business trip. "Your return flight leaves at eight-fifteen on Friday morning."

"I've never heard of the Brown Palace. Is it a decent place?"

"You don't remember our trip three years ago?" She sounded peeved. "Oh, right," she added sarcastically, "you don't remember anything before the coma except for what *Brad* did."

I held both hands out, palms up in a what-can-I-say gesture.

"Yes, it's a nice place. It's got a five-star rating and rivals the Ritz-Carlton in décor and service."

"Wow, fancy," I blurted, bouncing on the bed a little, earning a glare from Hilary. "I've never stayed in a place like that. I usually do the Motel 6-thing, or some other reasonably cheap motel."

"Yes, I'm sure *Brad* would do that. But *we* can afford to stay in the best hotels. And *we* do."

"I'm sure I can suffer through a couple of nights of luxury then." I bounced once more, just for the fun of it.

An evil grin appeared on her lips. "You know, I thought about going with you."

I jumped to my feet. My heart almost stopped beating. *No,* I screamed in my mind, *please, no.*

She suppressed a wicked chuckle. "But then, I realized this is something you need to do on your own. I didn't want to be in the way."

My shoulders dropped. Relief flooded through me. *I*

*need to stay calm. She's just messing around with my mind.* I knew she was looking at this trip as a way to prove I was Greg. I was going to prove her wrong.

She glared at me and started to say something. For a moment, I thought she'd read my mind. She shook her head slightly in exasperation and turned to leave. She paused at the door. "Martin will have the car here at six on Wednesday."

"Martin?"

"The limo driver."

"Oh, right. I didn't get his name last week when he drove me here from the nursing home. Wait a minute . . . six? That's only going to give me an hour to get from the house to the airport and through security. I think you'd better have him here at five."

"Security? You don't have to go through security."

"Since when?"

"We've never had to go through security. Martin drops us off at the plane. We get on and leave."

I sat down on the bed again. "Wait a minute. Is this a commercial flight?"

She gave me a disgusted look. "What do you think?"

"Okay, this makes sense now. You always fly on private planes, right?"

"Not planes, jets. And yes, we always fly private."

"This should be interesting," I said, fiddling with one of the straps on my bag.

"Oh, and I almost forgot." She reached into her pocket and pulled out some cash. Five one-hundred dollar bills. "Here's some cash for emergencies. You have plenty of credit cards, but we always like to carry extra cash for unexpected situations that might warrant it."

"Thanks." The cash was more than welcomed since I still wasn't comfortable using Greg's credit cards. Added to the cash that I still had in Greg's wallet, I would have plenty for my trip.

From another pocket, Hillary pulled out a cell phone and a charging cord. Handing them to me, she said, "Here is a cell phone for you to take with you. I programmed it with my personal cell number and the house number. This is a new cell phone, not your old personal cell phone, which contained all those business numbers and the numbers of your parents. I'm sure you don't want them pestering you on the trip."

"Thanks. I appreciate that. I'm sure this will come in handy." I placed it on the bed next to me. A post-it stuck on the back of the phone had the number of the phone written on it.

She sighed in resignation. "Hold down the number one and it will automatically dial my cell phone. Make sure you use it to keep me apprised of your plans." She abruptly turned and went out the door.

*An umbilical to home.* I picked up the phone and cord and threw them in my bag.

# Chapter 21

Denver, CO

$A$s Martin pulled the limo onto the tarmac and up to the plane, a woman walked down the steps leading up into the plane. Young, short and petite, she looked like a typical flight attendant. Her uniform consisted of dark blue slacks and a white shirt with gold trim on the sleeves. Her dark brown hair was secured in a ponytail by a red scrunchie.

Martin hurried out of the car and opened the door for me. I could have opened my own door, but I figured I might as well let him and these other people treat me like I was rich and famous.

"Hello, I'm Darcy. Welcome to Galaxy Airways," the attendant said as I got out of the car. "Do you have any baggage today?"

"Just a small carry-on," I told her as I held it up.

"Great. Follow me." She turned and started up the stairs. "You look familiar. Have you flown with us before?"

"Um . . . possibly. But if I did, I don't remember it." I knew Greg had flown a lot so he'd probably flown with them.

"Then I'll tell you a little about the plane. Our aircraft today is a Cessna Citation CJ4. It has a maximum cruising speed of 519 miles per hour and a range of about

2100 miles. You're the only passenger today, so you can sit anywhere you want." She ducked her head in the doorway and entered the plane.

Following her, I stopped inside to let my eyes adjust and look over the cabin. "Wow, very nice."

Across from the entry door was a leather sofa. Three leather-covered, high-backed captain-type chairs sat on the same side. Three additional chairs sat on the opposite side. Carpeted floors, upholstered walls, and fake wood molding added a touch of elegance to the look. Tall windows down both sides of the plane would give me ample opportunity to look down at the ground as we flew along.

The first two seats on each side faced backwards. I bypassed them and took the first front-facing seat on the right-hand side of the plane. I'd only flown a few times in the past. Never first class. Certainly, never on a private jet.

Darcy took my bag and put it in one of the storage bins. "Is there anything I can get for you before we take off?"

"I think I'm good for now. I might have a drink later though."

She laughed. "Then I'd better get it for you now. I'm not going to come out of the cockpit just to get you a drink."

It took me a second to realize what she'd meant. "Wait a minute," I gasped. "You're the pilot?"

"Pilot Darcy, at your service." She stood at attention and saluted me. "You have a problem with that?" she asked with a slight smile on her face.

"No . . . no I don't. I'm sorry," I said, feeling like a fool. "I thought you were a flight attendant."

"No problem. People make that mistake all the time. But on these small planes, we don't have attendants, at least most of the time. And with only one person on board, we never have one."

"Okay then," I said. "I guess I'll have a water or soda, whatever you have handy."

She walked to the front of the plane. Stopping just before the cockpit, she opened a door and pulled two bottles of water out of a small refrigerator. Bringing them back to me, she said, "If you've got everything you need, I'll get you buckled in. Then I'll go get us in the air."

She handed me the waters and I set them in the cup holders on the arm of the chair. After making sure my seat belt was fastened correctly, she said, "You saw where the fridge is. There are sandwiches, cheeses, smoked salmon, and fruits available. Snacks are in the cupboard above the fridge. Help yourself. The bathroom is that door." She pointed to a door with a universal restroom sign on it. "During the flight, I'd prefer it if you stayed in your seat with your seat belt done up. If you need to go to the bathroom or get food, do it quickly. The weather report shows a lot of turbulence along our flight path. I'd hate to hit a strong downdraft and have you plastered on the ceiling for a moment or two."

"I'm sure that wouldn't be fun," I replied.

"Being sucked up and plastered on the ceiling isn't the worst part," she added. "Slamming onto the floor when I correct the plane is the part that sucks." She gave me a lopsided grin. "You ready?"

Maybe she was kidding about correcting the plane so fast that I would slam into the floor, but then again, maybe she wasn't. Before we took off, I went to the bathroom and made sure I had plenty to eat and drink during the long flight to Denver. It didn't take long for me to get settled in my seat with everything I needed. "I'm set, Darcy," I called out. "Let 'er rip."

\* \* \*

As the plane came into Denver International Airport for a landing, I was already planning my next move, which was renting a car. The town of Golden, where my parents lived, was on the other side of Denver, about forty miles to the west of the airport.

I'd eaten on the plane and taken a short nap, so as soon as I arranged for a rental car, I could go straight to my parents' house.

A Lexus and a Jeep Grand Cherokee pulled up to the plane as I walked down the steps. A young man wearing a polo shirt with the Hertz logo on it got out of the Lexus. He walked back to the Jeep for a moment, then he walked up to me.

"Which car would you like, sir?" he asked, holding out two sets of keys.

Once again, Hilary was way ahead of me. "I think . . . the Jeep."

He handed me the keys. "Have a good day, sir." He turned, walked away, and waved as he climbed into the passenger seat of the Lexus.

"You're all set." Darcy held her hand out to me and we shook. "Thanks for flying with us. I hope you have a good time in Denver."

"Thanks. I hope this trip to Denver turns out to be good, too. It could be a life-changing trip."

She looked like she was on the verge of asking me what I meant, but instead, she turned and went back up the stairs to the plane.

I threw my bag on the back seat of the Jeep. Settling myself into the leather driver's seat, I fired up the engine and put it in drive. A large exit sign pointed the way out of the airport.

Driving through Denver, I saw changes I didn't remember. A building here, a car lot there. It made me feel . . . unsettled. I grew up in this area, I should have remembered all these things, especially the things that looked like they had been there for a long time.

The buildings were different, not what I remembered in my mind. I had a different vision of what should be there, compared to what I was really seeing now.

An ominous feeling settled over me. I couldn't help but wonder, briefly, if Hilary and the doctors were right. Maybe I really was Greg. "*No*," I shouted, gripping the steering wheel tightly. "I'm Brad Jones. I know I am. I remember my life. I have a family that lives here. I have a life in Havasu. I. Am. Brad. Jones."

I had to remain positive. I pushed the negative thoughts out of my mind and let my mind wander back over my life, concentrating on happy memories from my past. Birthdays as a kid. Snowy Christmas mornings with my parents. The times, both good and bad, I'd spent with Megan and her mother.

More recent memories of my time in Havasu with Chrissy floated across my mind. I thought about how much fun we had together and how much I loved her. All these memories of her I could definitely remember. They were so clear. At the same time, I didn't even have to try to remember anything from Greg's past. I knew, without a doubt, that no matter how hard I tried, I would never be able to remember anything from his past . . . because I wasn't Greg. I was Brad. Brad Jones. And at this moment, I was only two blocks from my childhood home.

\* \* \*

I pulled up to the curb in front of my parents' house. Dad used to get mad when anyone parked in the single-car driveway and blocked him in. So I was surprised to see, not one, but two cars parked in the driveway. I didn't recognize either.

Looking at the house, a chill raced across my skin. I had to admit, the house seemed to have some differences since the last time I'd seen it, almost a year ago. The light-blue paint with white trim that I'd helped my dad paint just last year, looked older and more worn than it should. Even from the curb, I could see the trim starting to flake and peel off.

The yard, surrounded by a shabby picket fence, was cluttered with leaves, branches from the decaying tree, and a few miscellaneous pieces of paper. The overgrown grass needed cutting and the weeds were climbing the fence. In short, I'd never seen the yard look so rundown. Mom and Dad were proud of their house and always took the extra time and effort to make it look tidy. I wondered if taking care of the house and yard was getting to be too much for them. Or maybe they'd been too busy lately to clean things up.

Overall, despite the wear and tear, the house and yard were familiar to me, including the layout of the trees and plants and the style and shape of the house. If I wasn't really Brad, and I hadn't grown up here, would I be able to fabricate this exact house in Greg's mind?

Hilary had told me that Greg traveled a lot for business. She didn't seem to know exactly where he went. So, even if he'd spent time in Denver on business, what were the chances that he would have come out here to Golden? To this exact house?

Well, maybe a business associate who lived here invited him to the house for dinner. I suppose something like that could have happened. It would explain why the house looked so familiar and yet not exactly like I remembered it from my last visit as Brad. I hated thinking these things. Was I second-guessing myself? Was I starting to think I might really be Greg? I just wasn't ready to give in by a long shot.

My first thought was to walk right up to the house and knock on the door. But if neither my mom nor my dad answered, then what? I had no idea.

I took a deep breath. Getting out of the car, I opened the gate and walked to the door. When I knocked, a small dog barked inside. A moment later, an older man opened the door about two inches. I could hear a game show blaring on the TV.

Surprisingly, I wasn't as shocked as I thought I'd be to see a stranger open the door of my parents' house.

"Yes?" he asked as he used a foot to keep the yapping dog from getting out and tearing my ankle to shreds.

An idea came to me suddenly. "Hi. Sorry to bother you, but I'm trying to track down lost relatives and this was the last address I could find for them. Are you Dick Jones?"

His face relaxed. He probably thought I was going to try to sell him something he didn't want. He seemed relieved that I only asked for information.

"Nope, I'm not. Never heard of him."

My heart fell. Suddenly I felt like I was in the Twilight Zone. "Oh, okay," I stammered. "Could he have lived here before you moved in?"

"Nope. The wife and I bought this house two years ago in an estate auction. Can't remember the name of the fellow who owned it, but it wasn't Jones." He turned and looked impatiently back into the house for a moment.

I glanced up and down the street as I wondered if I was wrong about the timing. *Has it been one or two years since I last saw my parents? Did they move out? Did they not tell me? But I called them, not that long ago. I have to be right.* "Do you think any of the neighbors would know of him?"

"I don't know. Guess you could ask, but most of them are at work." He looked into the house again. "I'm missing my show. Can you go now?"

Nothing like being abrupt. "Sure, thanks for taking the time to talk to me. Have a good day."

The door shut in my face.

I stumbled back to my car as another car pulled out from across the street and headed slowly past me. I couldn't get my head around the thought that everyone might be right about me being Greg. It just couldn't be. I put the car into gear and focused on checking the homes of my sister and Megan. I decided to go to Megan's first, since she had an apartment in Golden.

On the drive, I had to give myself several pep talks. Finding someone else living in my parent's house had brought on a growing bout of depression. I had to keep my chin up and keep plugging ahead. The only other alternative was giving in and becoming Greg. Not an option. Brad could never live the life that Greg lived.

Ten minutes later, I pulled up in front of Megan's apartment building. It looked somewhat like I remembered, except it was a lot smaller a complex and more rundown than I was expecting. When I knocked on Megan's door, the young couple living there had never heard of her and said they'd been living there for three years.

Now, I was really starting to panic. If my parents weren't living in their house, where were they? Did they exist? What about Megan? Where would she have gone? What if I couldn't find my family, everyone I cared about and who made my life worth living? I was too confused to think about the implications of all this right now. I had one more place to check.

My sister's house was located within the city limits of Denver, not very far from Golden. Right away, I could tell it wasn't worth walking up to the door. The house had been turned into a day-care center. The sign on the wooden fence said they had been in business for ten years. The house and yard showed it, too.

Another disappointment. A feeling of grief and loss washed over me. Had I lost all my family? And worse, the nagging worry that everyone else was right about me being Greg got stronger. I felt crushed and torn inside.

*   *   *

It was now close to two o'clock in the afternoon. Check-in time at the Brown Palace was not until three.

I pulled into the parking lot of a mom and pop coffee shop that didn't look too busy. After getting seated in a booth, I ordered a burger and fries. The restaurant owners had put newspapers in every booth, I thought it was a nice touch. While I ate in silence, I read some articles in the paper. It kept my mind momentarily distracted.

After the dishes were removed, I sat nursing a cup of coffee and a shaky belief in what I had thought was rock solid. How could this be happening? Where was the family that left me with so many real memories of a wonderful life?

Was I really Greg? If I was Greg, why couldn't I remember anything about that life? I mean, Greg had it all: a beautiful wife, three kids, a luxurious house, and lots of money. Well, the wife was a tad cold and overbearing. The kids seemed a little screwed-up. The parents were off-the-wall crazy. But, the house was nice. And Greg didn't have any money problems. I got the impression he was a hard worker and excellent businessman.

Living Greg's life from the inside for the last week had left me cold. Hilary left me cold. Some of that money would certainly come in handy, but one family having so much wealth seemed unnatural to me. I didn't think I would like having that much money with all the responsibilities involved. It seemed too complicated. It wasn't who I thought myself to be.

Another thought came to me. Did Greg like his life? Was it possible that he hated his life so much, his mind created an alternate life? One with loving, caring parents, a sister who would do anything for him, the perfect daughter. A life with a good job he enjoyed doing, a town where the weather was almost always warm, a dog to welcome him home after a hard day's work. A life with the girlfriend of his dreams who was his best friend. Brad's life. My life.

I wondered if it was possible for Greg to have created this life during his coma. Or, what if he had created it in his mind while he was living an unhappy life in New York, like a fantasy in his spare time? Maybe he had given it so much detail that, when he went into the coma, the fantasy life took over. He could have used Google Earth to explore Denver and Lake Havasu, picking out imaginary houses and places he'd worked, making up his own story as he went.

That might explain how I knew so much about Denver and Golden, even though the reality of the locations weren't what I had pictured in my mind. Greg could have built a complete imaginary life to help him cope with a life he hated and was stuck in. The more I thought about it, the more it made sense. With a little internet research, anyone could learn about almost anything. Greg's imaginary life, my life, could have taken over his mind before he came out of the coma. It made sense in a weird kind of way. I didn't know if such a thing was possible or not.

The idea of Greg creating his own world wasn't exactly thrilling to me. If it was true, I would have to admit to Hilary she was right and I really was Greg. And worse, she would be my wife! I married her. Those kids would be my children. My parents were stiff and cold. *Oh, my god, it just couldn't be.*

This whole line of thinking was getting a little too deep and scary for me. I idly wondered what Doctor Morrison would say about all this.

What still hurt was the fact that the parents, sister, and daughter I had loved were out of my reach. Even if I had made them up, they were truly dear to me and a painful loss.

I had an idea. I caught the waitress's attention and waved her over. "Would you have a phone book I can borrow for a minute?"

"Sure, I'll be right back."

Now I was glad Hilary had given me the cell phone. I had three calls to make.

When the waitress brought me the phone book, I opened it to the business pages. I couldn't find the listing I wanted. Then I remembered a few years back the official name of the company became Molson Coors. I found the number and dialed. An automated answering system responded and I pressed the number given for Human Relations.

"Molson Coors Human Relations," a female voice said. "How may I help you?"

"My name is Brad Jones. I was adopted as a baby and I'm trying to track down relatives. Did you have a Richard Jones working there? I believe he retired five years ago. He went by Dick. He would—"

"I'm sorry, sir, but I can't give out information about employees without the proper paperwork being filled out and filed with the Employment Division."

"I don't want information," I said. "I just want to know if he worked there."

"Well, since I won't be giving you any information, I guess I could tell you if he ever worked here or not." Her computer keys clicked over the phone. "I don't show anyone by that name ever working for our company. Are you sure that is the correct name?"

"Yes, I'm sure. Thank you for looking." Not encouraging.

I set the phone on the table and opened the phone book again. *One down, two to go.* I looked up the number of Megan's job and dialed.

"Hello, this is Megan. How may I help you?"

I froze. Did she say Megan? Could it be? Could my search be coming to an end? If it is her, does—

"Hello? Is anyone there?"

"Oh, sorry. I was startled for a minute there. Did you say your name was Megan?"

"Yes, it is. How may I help you?"

"Would your last name happen to be Jones?"

She was silent for a moment, then said, "No, it's Finch."

I hadn't realized how tense I'd grown until I felt myself deflate at her words. "Is there a Megan Jones who works there?"

"No," she replied suspiciously. "Why are you calling?"

"Oh, I'm sorry. I was adopted when I was a baby and I'm tracking down people who may be related to me. I was told that a Megan Jones worked there."

"No, I've been here for ten years and I know all the employees. We've never had another Megan here. I'm sorry. I hope you find your relatives."

"Thanks. I hope so, too." I hung up and took a sip of my coffee. *Not looking good. One more to go.*

I dreaded making this call: my sister's workplace. Unfortunately, I got the same response. She'd never been there. *Strike three.* I couldn't have felt more mournful than if I had just attended a funeral of my whole family.

"Would you like more coffee?" the waitress asked, interrupting my thoughts.

It suddenly hit me. "No thanks. I've got to go. I've got a long drive ahead of me."

"Oh, yeah," she said out of curiosity, "where ya goin'?"

"Home, I hope."

As she walked away uninterested, I dialed the phone number I got from the tag on the keys for the car rental company. I thought they might argue or be upset that I wanted to take the Jeep to Arizona. Instead, they said there was no problem and that I could return the Jeep to any of their outlets. I didn't know if that was standard procedure or if it was because of the name on the credit card. *Money does have its privileges,* I thought, as I headed out for the most important part of my journey.

# Chapter 22

## Lake Havasu City, AZ

By the time I got out of Denver, it was late in the afternoon. It would be a fourteen-hour drive to Havasu, more than I wanted to do in one shot, so I figured I'd stop somewhere along the way and sleep for a few hours. Before leaving Denver, I had stopped at a store and bought a foam pad and a lightweight sleeping bag to lay out in the back of the Jeep.

On the long drive, I had a lot of time to think about everything. It weighed heavy on my mind that it had only taken me a few hours in Denver to prove my parents, my sister, and my daughter were not there. It pained me to think that maybe they had never been there. What if I hadn't searched hard enough? I second-guessed myself and almost turned around more than once. But then, the phone calls to the places they had worked seemed like pretty solid evidence against me.

Even though I didn't find a trace of my parents, daughter, or sister, I felt compelled to look for the final threads of Brad's life in Havasu. That's where my strongest bond lay, and I held a lot of hope that it would resolve all my fears and answer all my questions. I had to know for sure who I was.

Around midnight, I stopped at a rest area in southern Utah to sleep. After folding down the rear seats, I was able to stretch out in the back on the foam pad and sleeping bag. Not the best bed I'd ever slept on, but not the worst either. Sure, I would have gotten a better night's sleep in the Brown Palace Hotel, but I was in a hurry. By sleeping in the Jeep, I was already half-way to Havasu.

As it turned out, I managed to get only about five hours of restless sleep. Rest areas were noisy. A steady stream of eighteen-wheelers, cars, and trucks came and went. Added to the vehicle noise were barking dogs, yelling adults, and noisy kids. After a while, I gave up on the sleep and headed for a truck stop where I ate a breakfast of coffee and donuts. Then, I was on the road again.

In Nevada, the sky started getting light. I marveled at the surrounding country. The early morning colors were brighter and more varied than any desert I'd ever seen. I'd been across this road before, but today the desert seemed more vibrant, full of life. It renewed my hope, at least temporarily, that all would turn out well.

I took a break in Vegas to stretch my legs, get more coffee, and use the restroom. The gas station also had a burger joint, a car wash, and slot machines. How nice. One-stop shopping.

Two more hours to Havasu. I took the Highway 95 cutoff south out of Boulder City. The towns and unique landmarks I passed looked vaguely familiar. Almost as if I'd seen them before, but a long, long time ago. Well, at least they looked sort of familiar.

The fear I'd kept at bay began to set in. Each mile I put behind me brought a little more worry about what I was going to find when I got into Havasu. After my discouraging discoveries in Denver, I was beginning to wonder why I was even going to Havasu. I didn't know if I could face more grief and loss.

At Exit Nine, I turned off I-40 onto Highway 95. A

sign said it was twelve miles to Havasu. *And about five miles ahead is where I got into a head-on collision and went into a coma. Somehow, I awoke in New York and started this crazy ride.*

Look as I might, I didn't see signs of any recent wrecks on the road. Of course, according to Hilary, Greg's accident had happened some five weeks ago, but in my life it hadn't been that long, like two weeks. I had expected to see skid marks or something left on the road.

Impatient and apprehensive, I sped up, ten-miles-per-hour over the speed limit. I had to force myself to calm down and slow down. The closer I got to Havasu, the more nervous I grew about what I would find. Every mile put me that much closer to finding out who I really was. Would it be Brad or Greg?

Arriving at the outskirts of Havasu, I passed the airport on my left. A Toyota dealership and a huge shopping complex with a Wal-Mart sat on the other side. Beyond the shopping center, I could see the upper end of the lake.

A few miles down the road, the speed limit changed as I came into the main part of town. I took a deep breath as I slowed down and looked around. I recognized some buildings and landmarks.

I drove all the way to the other end of town, still looking for things that matched the memories in my mind. The town seemed slightly different than what I had pictured, but it wasn't as disappointing as it could have been, It was close enough and familiar enough that I felt a sense of relief.

As far as Hilary knew, Greg had never been here, so I didn't have any of his memories to build on. Therefore, by my reasoning, I had been here before. Which meant I was Brad Jones.

\* \* \*

The first thing I did was drive to my house. As it came into view, I intended to rush inside and check on Sadie. But when I saw various unknown vehicles parked out front, one being a boat, I restrained myself and slowed down. Strange people stood in the driveway and went in and out of my house, which was a light stucco grey, not the earthy southwestern tan color I remembered. The landscaping had been changed, too. I'd spent a lot of time putting in trees and plants, I even designed a rock river. Instead, crushed landscape rock filled this yard, with a couple of ratty-looking cacti scattered around. I drove past the house and parked out of sight down the street, trying to stop my heart from pounding in my chest.

When I got my bearings, I dared to drive to the apartment where Chrissy had lived. I sat outside, watching the building for a long time. Finally, I rang the doorbell. Sweat began to run down my face as I stood there waiting.

The door of another apartment opened a crack. "What you want?" The speaker sounded like an older Asian woman.

"I'm looking for a woman named Chrissy." I turned so the woman could see my face better and maybe allay her fears.

"Clarence live there, alone. He gone to store."

"Do you know if a young lady named Chrissy lives in one of these other apartments?" I waved my hand, indicating the other ten or so apartments in the complex.

"No. Everyone live here older. Retired. Except one couple and baby."

"Okay," I said as a cloud of gloom dropped over me. "Thanks for the information."

As I walked toward the Jeep, I asked myself why I thought I would be lucky enough to find Chrissy here when every other search had been a failure. Despite that, just for one more try, I went to the store where she worked, but that was a dead end, too.

It took me a while to shake myself out of a stupor of sadness and uneasiness. How could Chrissy not be real? I loved her. We loved each other. My heart ached. And worse, I did not want to think about the complications of being Greg or what I was going to do next.

I spent the rest of the morning driving around town, looking for places I recognized. It was strange, some buildings and areas looked familiar, yet in small, subtle ways, they were also unfamiliar.

I drove by one of the last houses I'd worked on. I definitely remembered that house because I had admired the landscape. It had three palm trees and a palo verde tree in the front yard. Today, it had one palm tree, Bougainvillea plants, and an ocotillo cactus. What made it confusing is that I remembered that the house was on a certain street and it looked somewhat familiar. That seemed important.

In the afternoon, I checked into a Motel 6. I could have used one of Greg's credit cards or cash to stay at the best hotel in town, but as Brad, Motel 6 felt more to my liking.

In the motel office, as one last recourse, I asked to see a phone book. I wanted to know if *Brad's Handyman & Remodeling Services* existed. Nothing. I looked through the local *White Sheet* classifieds where I used to place ads. Nothing there, either.

I walked to my motel room with a heavy heart.

# Chapter 23

## Lake Havasu City, AZ

Early Friday morning, I called Hilary on my cell phone. I hated having to call her because I would have to admit she had been right, but I knew if I didn't call, she'd eventually call me. In fact, I was surprised she hadn't already called. I was sure she was curious to know what I had discovered.

I pressed and held number one. It automatically dialed a number.

"Good morning, Gregory," Hilary said in a business-like voice. Greg's name must have come up on her caller ID.

I pictured her sitting at the kitchen table, fully dressed, makeup and hair already done up for the day. A cup of tea and a croissant or a bagel with butter and jelly sat in front of her as breakfast. *Nothing changes,* I thought. *She does that every morning.* Wait a minute. I didn't even want to think about how I knew this information about her, but I did. Not good. Score one for Greg's memory.

"Good morning to you, too, Hilary."

"So how is the search going, hmmm? Have you found your long-lost parents yet?" Her voice dripped with sarcasm.

"No, I haven't." I noticed she avoided saying anything about Megan or Chrissy.

Without emotion, she said, "I'm sorry, Gregory. I know how hard this must be for you. I'm sure you'll get over it in time."

Because of her indifference, I couldn't resist adding, "I haven't found my daughter Megan nor my girlfriend Chrissy, either."

"Your girlfriend?"

"Ummm, listen, I'm . . . "

"Don't beat around the bush, Gregory," she snapped. "If you have something to say, say it."

"I just wanted to let you know . . . I'm in Lake Havasu. I couldn't come back to New York until I—"

"I know where you are," she said bitterly. "I called the Brown Palace Hotel last night to talk to you. When they said you didn't show up, I called the car rental company. I should have expected this, really. It's so . . . so . . . Brad."

She always managed to push my buttons. My anger flared. I stood up and stormed to the window. "Yeah, it is something I would do, isn't it? I'll bet Greg wouldn't have dared do anything like this. He—"

"Come now, Gregory. Don't talk that way. Gregory wouldn't have to sneak around trying to find an imaginary girlfriend to make him feel complete. I can't wait until you revert back to him. Brad is such a . . . ."

"What am I, Hilary? A hick? A redneck? A common man?" I was growing more and more pissed, stomping around the room. It was a good thing I was on the ground floor so nobody below me would have to listen to me tromp back and forth across the floor.

"Calm down, Gregory. You don't want—"

"I'll tell you what I don't want, Hilary. I don't want to come back there. Not for a few days. I'm going to spend some time here, see if I can find anyone here who knows me. I'm taking a break to try to figure out what to do next."

She didn't respond right away. I wondered if she'd hung up.

In a voice that could have flash frozen a fish swimming in warm tropical water, she said, "That's fine. Take your time. I'm sure that you'll find the same thing you found in Denver. I'll cancel your return flight. Call if you want me to arrange your flight home. Have a nice day."

I sat there in stunned silence. I'd never met anyone who could change moods so fast. "Listen, Hilary, I'm sorry, but you've got to let me figure this out on my own. Until I can deal with this duel life, I'm going to need some space."

Silence again.

I pulled the phone away from my ear and looked at the screen. The call had been terminated. I didn't know when she'd hung up. I didn't know if she'd heard my last words. It didn't matter though. I didn't care what she thought. I was going to do what I needed to do and there wasn't a damn thing she could do about it.

* * *

Before I'd met Chrissy, I had belonged to a few different clubs and organizations in town. I was a member of the Elks Lodge, the Eagles Lodge, and the local Gem and Mineral Society. I had been involved with a hiking group and a kayaking group and, at one time, I had been on a baseball team.

I spent the day driving and walking around town while looking for people I might recognize. I went into grocery stores, strip-mall shops, department stores, and restaurants. I wandered through the local Rotary Park and through the shops along the walk under the London Bridge. After a frustrating day of not seeing anyone I knew, I gave up and went back to my room.

It was Friday night. I decided to go the Elks Lodge and give it another try. Since I didn't have a membership card, I couldn't get in on my own. I'd need a member to sign me in. So, I stood off to the side of the main entrance door and eyed prospective victims. After about ten minutes of standing in the heat of the early evening, I watched a couple holding hands and heading for the door. I thought this might be my best shot.

The man wore a cowboy hat, jeans, and a western shirt. The woman wore tight jeans with sparkling jewels on the sides of the pockets and a lacy feminine top. Her short blond hair had been cut in a pixie style. They both wore rings so I took it they were man and wife.

"Excuse me," I said, stepping toward them.

"Can we help you with something?" the cowboy asked, stepping just in front of his wife as if he was protecting her from me.

"Well," I replied, "I'm new in town and I'm interested in joining the Lodge. I'd like to check it out before I join, but I understand that I can't go inside unless I'm a member. Someone else has to take me in as a guest."

The cowboy stared hard at me. "And you want us to take you in, right?"

"Would you mind?"

They looked at each other for a second, then he shrugged and said, "Sure, why not?"

"Great. By the way, I'm Brad Jones." I held out my hand.

"Brad Jones . . . ," the woman said as she studied me. "Why does that sound familiar?"

My heart jumped to my throat. Did she know me? Did I know her? She didn't look familiar. Maybe she'd been a client, but I didn't think so. I remembered almost everyone I'd done a job for, and I was pretty sure I hadn't done one for her. Of course, she could know *of* me from someone else? Maybe she was a friend of someone I'd worked for and they had mentioned my name to her.

She turned to her husband. "Wasn't that the name of the mechanic who repaired our car?"

"No. That was Bill Jinks."

"Oh, that's right," she said.

Hiding my disappointment, I asked, "So, you'll take me in as your guest?"

"Sure," the cowboy said. "I'm Ed. This is Leda."

"Nice to meet you, Leda."

"Nice to meet you, too," Leda said, fanning herself. "It's hot out here. Can we go inside?"

"After you," Ed replied as he slipped his membership card into the reader and opened the door.

The sounds of a bar assaulted my ears as we stepped inside. A man sitting on a stool just inside the door checked Ed's membership card and had him sign me in. We walked through the bar to get to the dining room. I remembered the bar as being different, in a separate room off to one side, but the dining room almost matched what I remembered.

As Ed led the way to a table, I noticed that the band stage sat in one corner with the dance floor rotated at a forty-five-degree angle to the walls. For some reason, I had thought the dance floor was set squarely against the end wall. We sat next to the dance floor and Ed made sure he sat with Leda on his right and me on his left. He seemed to be a little over-cautious about me, being a stranger.

It was still early for the Friday night life, so only about twenty or twenty-five people sat around the place at tables. An entertainer wearing a faded white cowboy hat was preparing his equipment on stage. A cocktail waitress came by and took our drink order. I ordered a beer. Ed and Leda ordered a picture of water.

The overhead lights made it easy to study the room,

and more importantly, to study the people in the room. I looked from face to face, trying to find someone familiar.

"Are you looking for someone?" Ed said suspiciously. "Maybe we shouldn't have brought you in here. You look like you're looking for someone." He slid back his chair and turned so he could face me directly. "Are you here to cause trouble?"

The waitress chose that moment to bring our drinks. I paid for my beer and knew I had to be careful what came out of my mouth next. "In a way, I am looking for someone. But not in a bad way." I told them a short version of my story.

Leda seemed interested the whole time and I felt she believed me. I wasn't sure about Ed.

The lights dimmed and the entertainer started playing music and singing. A few people, including Ed and Leda, got up to dance. I watched them move around the dance floor and was mesmerized by their fancy steps and Leda's graceful twirls. In between, I looked at the faces of the other dancers and guests, but saw no one I knew.

When Ed and Leda came back to the table, I couldn't help but say, "Wow, you two are really good dancers. Wasn't that what they call a two-step?"

Ed took a long drink of water. "Thanks, and yes, that was a two-step. We used to teach the two-step and the country waltz, but we got burned out. We haven't danced for a few years. We just started coming back out about a month ago. We're a little rusty."

"So, did you see anyone you know?" Leda asked.

"No, not yet," I said. "Maybe when more people get here I'll get lucky."

They jumped up to dance again, leaving me to watch for someone I might recognize. As new individuals and couples entered the dining room, I grew more and more discouraged. In my mind, I had been here at the Elks about three months ago. Chrissy and I had come out for dinner and a little dancing. We didn't come here a lot, but often enough that I felt I ought to have recognized at least a few people. But that wasn't the case.

For a while, I noticed one man, sitting by himself with a mug of beer, kept looking at me, or at least kept looking in my direction. Every time I shifted my head to look back at him, he turned away. Even seated in a chair, he looked tall and lanky. He wore a scruffy beard. He didn't seem familiar. Maybe he thought he knew me or something. I kept an eye on him, but eventually, he appeared to ignore me.

After a couple hours, Ed stood up and said, "Well, we're done for the night. Since we brought you in as our guest, I'm afraid you'll have to leave with us, too."

"Not a problem. I'm not seeing anyone I know. But I really appreciate you bringing me in."

"You're welcome," Leda said with a smile. "I hope you find someone who can help you."

"Me, too."

We made our way outside and said our goodbyes.

I got in the Jeep and sat there for a while, pondering the incongruity of so many things and places being familiar and unfamiliar at the same time.

Rather than driving straight to the motel, I turned the key in the ignition and took a detour. *Tomorrow will be different,* I told myself as I drove past Chrissy's apartment.

# Chapter 24

## Lake Havasu City, AZ

I woke up Sunday morning to the sun coming into my room through the blinds. If I remembered right, a huge outdoor swap meet, the famous London Bridge Swap Meet, was held every Sunday in Lake Havasu between Labor Day and Memorial Day. This would be another test of my memories.

While I lay in bed, I mulled over the day before. With the exception of visiting the Eagles Lodge instead of the Elks, Saturday had turned out to be a carbon copy of Friday. Right down to the tall bearded man who was paying so much attention to me.

He had entered the Eagles Lodge a short time after I arrived and sat where I was in his line of view. He tried to be inconspicuous about it, but it wasn't hard to tell he was watching me with his eyes wandering my way all the time. Then he'd turn when I looked straight at him.

One of the managers, sitting at the front door, signed me in on the pretense that I was thinking of becoming a member.

When I was ready to leave for the evening, I had asked the manager, "Do you know who that man is?" I pointed to the man with the beard.

"He looks familiar, but I don't know his name. Why do you want to know?"

"The guy looks like someone I knew once. I was just curious as to who he is."

As far as other people who I might have known in my past life, the results were the same: nada. My life as Brad seemed to have disappeared. It was too painful to think about on this beautiful Sunday morning, so I got out of bed and dressed to go out for breakfast.

From Motel 6, I walked to IHOP for a light breakfast. Being that these two buildings were adjacent to the parking lot where the swap meet was held, I felt a kind of self-satisfied relief to see many open booths and canopies already set up by vendors. I was happy that this memory was real and I didn't dare question how I knew.

Luckily for me, everything was in walking distance, so I didn't have to worry about parking, which was a premium for the crowds who came to buy or wander through the aisles.

After breakfast at IHOP, I headed for the swap meet, entering at the southeast corner. The sun was shining and the temperature was a mild seventy degrees, with no wind. A beautiful October day in Havasu.

I stepped off to the side and paused to look around. The London Bridge Swap Meet was held on a huge parking lot, surrounded by businesses, most of which were closed on Sundays. The vendors purchased parking spots for their booths. Most had pop-up canopies. Some placed their wares on tables while others simply set everything on the ground. All kinds of wears were sold: hand-crafted items like pottery, jewelry, walking sticks, and art; wind chimes, sun glasses, hats and shirts, books, and tools; even stun guns.

A number of booths promoted local businesses, like realtors, construction companies, vehicle retailers, sun screens, and many more. A number of vendors sold used garage-sale items. It was a great place to find all kinds of deals.

In my mind, I used to love walking through the aisles every Sunday. I never knew what kind of bargain I might find. But being here now, it seemed different. I didn't recognize any of the vendors. I wondered if I really had spent that much time here. *On the other hand, it feels like home.*

I headed up the first row. Then, I hit the second and the third rows. Although a lot of the merchandise looked familiar, none of the vendors I used to talk to were there. By the time I was halfway through the swap meet, a growing feeling of depression started to take over. *Don't stop now*, I told myself. *Don't give up*. I continued on.

I shouldn't have been surprised, but by the time I got to the last row on the lake side, I stood in a daze of mixed emotions, wondering again how the familiar and unfamiliar feelings played into this reality that I had lived.

"Are you all right?" a voice said.

I snapped out of my daze to see a blond-haired older woman staring at me with her hands on her hips.

"What? . . . Oh, yeah, sure," I replied.

"Ya sure?" Her blue eyes narrowed in concern. She stared hard at me for a moment, trying to figure out if I was lying or not.

In her booth, I saw a cooler with a sign advertising water for a dollar a bottle. "Could I buy a water from you?" I asked, hoping to get off the subject of how I was feeling. It was like I'd just woken up from a deep sleep. Not seeing any familiar vendors had hit me harder than I thought. I needed a moment to gather myself and get back on track.

"Sure, follow me." She turned and walked to the cooler.

I pulled a dollar out of my wallet and traded it for the water. I glanced around at the contents of her booth as I took a drink. There were no canopies here, just tables filled with . . . stuff. Old books, toys, and glassware dominated a lot of the tables. Miscellaneous items like old cigar boxes, tools, and knick-knacks filled the rest of the tables in her booth. A wetsuit and a rack of old license plates hung from a telephone pole. A music box played country music at a nice, mellow volume.

A tall man with a goatee was making change for a customer. As he finished, he hurried to the side of the woman who was helping me. He grabbed her and gave her a big bear hug and then a kiss as he said, "There she is. The most beautiful woman in the world."

The woman laughed and slapped his shoulder. "Let me go. I'm talking to this nice man." She nodded her head sideways toward me. She pushed herself away from the man and put her hand to her mouth, only partly covering a fake grin. In a loud whisper, she said to her husband, "I think he's a little confused."

"Really?" He looked at me with a serious eye.

"I'm fine. Really, I am," I said. "I just have a lot on my mind today. And I wasn't paying attention to where I was going. But . . . can I ask you a question?"

"See, I told you he was confused."

The man gave her a dark look. "Be quiet. Let's see what he wants."

"Have you two been doing the swap meet very long?"

The man looked at his wife and shrugged. "What . . . two . . . three years?"

"About that," she replied. "By the way. I'm Nancy. This is Gene."

I shook their hands. "Brad. Brad Jones."

Nancy cocked her head to the side and said, "I've got a funny feeling there's more going on with you than meets the eye. Come clean. What's up?"

They seemed like a trustworthy couple. I decided to tell them a little about my problem. I said, "It's interesting you mentioned *funny feelings*." I told them my story.

When I got done, Gene said, "No wonder you're so out of it. I would be, too."

"Is there anything we can do for you?" Nancy asked.

"No, I don't think so. I think I've done just about everything I can do here. I guess it's time to go back to New York and . . . " I couldn't finish saying it.

"You're not convinced you can live as Greg, are you?" Gene asked.

Nancy playfully slapped Gene in the belly. "Of course, he isn't. He really believes he's Brad. Would you be happy going to New York and living a life you hated?"

He laughed. "No."

Nancy turned serious. "I think you need to stay here, at least another day or two. Think about your options. You never know, you might decide to stay for good."

"I don't know. I feel like I've done all I can do. But then again, I don't really want to go . . . back there."

Nancy winked at me. "Give it a few days. You never know what might happen."

"You're right. I'll do that." I noticed people milling around in the booth, eyeing us, seeming to need help. "I better go. You've got customers who need your help."

"Okay," Gene said, "but if you're here next week, stop by and say hello."

"For sure," Nancy said.

"I will. Thanks."

They waved and headed off to help their customers.

Me, I wandered back to the motel. Instead of going to the room, I got into the Jeep, rolled the windows down, and sat there wondering what to do. Should I stay in town another day or two, or not? Really, I couldn't see the sense in staying. After failing to find my family in Golden and failing to find Chrissy here, what was there for me? I saw no reason to stay, other than it would delay my return to New York and to Hilary.

I leaned my head on the steering wheel and closed my eyes. What should I do? All my plans to prove I was Brad had failed. I didn't know where to turn. I guess I just wasn't ready to turn to Hilary. I took a deep breath and decided to stay in town at least one more day.

It was late morning. The swap meet was open for three or four more hours, so I decided to go back through the aisles once more. I picked up a couple of little items at a bargain price. I passed by the wares of Gene and Nancy, but they were so busy with customers, I didn't want to bother them.

At one point, I thought I saw the tall man who had been watching me at the Elks and at the Eagles. I didn't see him clearly, just a glimpse through the crowd, but I was pretty sure it was the same guy. At first, I wondered if he was following me. I couldn't imagine why. Hilary knew where I was and she certainly had no reason to have me followed. As Brad, I seemed to be a stranger to everyone else in town. In the end, I put it down to coincidence and forgot about it.

The comfortable seventy-degree temperature of earlier this morning was gone. It was getting hot now that the sun was high in the sky. Since I'd eaten a light breakfast, my stomach started growling. A Del Taco happened to sit in the vicinity, across the street from the IHOP. A burger, fries, a burrito, and a tall, ice-cold drink in a cool restaurant sounded pretty good to me.

I walked to the restaurant, opened the door, and came face to face with Chrissy.

# Chapter 25

Lake Havasu City, AZ

Chrissy now wore her hair longer than she liked to wear it. It was lighter in color, too, as though the golden highlights of her auburn hair made her almost blond. But other than that, she looked exactly the same as the last time I'd seen her. She even wore shorts and a tank top, just like she used to wear when we'd go to the swap meet together.

I couldn't believe my eyes. I blurted, "Oh, my god, Chrissy? Is that you? It's me, Brad."

She looked at me like I was a wild-eyed freak out to torment young women. "Um, no. Excuse me." She hurried past me and out the door. She carried her to-go bag of food tightly in one hand and her car keys in the other.

"No, wait," I said desperately. "I need to talk to you." I followed her from a little distance. I didn't want her to think I was going to attack her or anything.

She looked over her shoulder with suspicion. Seeing me following, she sped up.

"It's a matter of life and death. Please . . . just give me two minutes of your time."

Keeping a careful eye on me, she quickly unlocked the door of a red car, slid into the driver's seat, and slammed the door shut.

I stepped up to the window. The car doors locked. "Please. Two minutes is all I ask."

She put her key in the ignition and started the car. From the look on her face, it was obvious she didn't recognize me.

*How could that be after all the time we'd spent together*? A moment of confusion washed over me. *Did we spend time together? Is this a Chrissy look-alike?* "Please," I begged.

She rolled her window down an inch. "Whose life?"

"What?"

"You said it was a matter of life and death. Whose life is in danger?"

*Crap, this could get messy real quick. How am I going to explain this in two minutes?* "Actually, two lives hang in the balance. Mine and a guy named Greg Nordmeyer."

She chuckled. "Nordmeyer?"

I smiled. "Bear with me and I'll explain everything."

"Okay, start talking. My food is getting cold and I have things to do."

"First, my name is Brad Jones." I saw no recognition at the mention of my name. Not good. "About three weeks ago, I was living here in Havasu with you."

She shook her head in disgust and started to roll her window up.

"No, wait. It will all make sense, I promise. Just let me explain, okay?"

She paused for a second, glanced at her food bag, then nodded her head.

"Three weeks ago, I was living here. Then I got into a car wreck. When I woke up, I found myself in New York state. They told me my name was Greg Nordmeyer. Suddenly, I had a life I didn't know, including a wife and three kids." I wasn't sure if it was because I was nervous or if it was because it was hot outside, but I was sweating. I knew I had to talk fast and be careful or I would lose her. "Listen, can we go inside? While you eat your food, I'll finish telling you my story. I promise, I'm not a freak and I won't hurt you. I just need to talk to you. To tell you my story."

She paused, watching me through the window as she thought about it.

I said a silent prayer, hoping she'd hear my story. Even if she just listened and left without believing it, at least I'd have spent some time with her. It hurt my soul so much that she didn't recognize me.

She smiled.

My heart melted. God, I loved this woman.

She chuckled. "Thanks. You've made my day. This is the best pick-up line I've ever heard. You really had me going. I can't wait to tell the girls at work. They'll die over this one."

I was crushed. She thought I was just trying to pick her up. Well, in a way, I could see how it looked like that. In her reality, she'd never seen me before today and I was coming on pretty strong. "I'm not giving you a line. I'm dead serious, Chrissy."

"One . . . my name isn't Chrissy. It's *Christy*. Two . . . if your story is really true, how come I don't remember you, or our so-called life together?"

"It's complicated. I think I might be Greg and that I hated my life so much, I made up an alternate life, our life. Somehow it took over my mind while I was in a coma."

She pursed her lips and scrunched her brows down in what I used to call her serious face. She only used it when she was thinking about something really hard. "I . . . I don't know. This all sounds so . . ."

"Unbelievable, I know." I stood there in frustration. *What do I do now?* "If you'll listen to me, I think I can explain it so that it will make sense to you."

She took a deep breath and looked around. She was fidgety, nervous.

Not a good sign. What more could I say? Either she'd come inside and listen to my story, or she wouldn't. It was her choice. I had to resign myself to that.

She looked me in the eye. "I'm sorry, but I don't think I want to hear your story. What happened to you, happened to you, not to me. If you are searching for a new life, and made up a *fake life* that had me in it, I'm sure you can find somebody else to replace me. I have to go now." She put the car in reverse.

I walked alongside the car as she backed out. "Think about what I've said. If you change your mind, I'll be at Motel 6 . . . room one-thirty-two . . . for the next two days. Call or come to the room. I'll be there."

Without looking at me, she stopped, put the car in drive, and drove away.

I stood there like an idiot in love. I don't know why I'd said I'd stay two days, but I felt I had to give her some time to think things over. Deep down, I wasn't sure if two days would be enough.

I watched the red car until it went out of sight. Would I ever see her again?

\* \* \*

The first thing I did in my motel room was to open the curtains wide so I could see people coming and going. If Chrissy, correction, Christy, showed up, I wanted to see her right away. If she came as far as my door, I wasn't going to let her get away again. I sat on the edge of the bed and watched. All the while, I wondered what I could have done better to make her stay at the restaurant and talk to me.

It interested me that her name, her looks, her

mannerisms, and her personality were so close to what I'd created in my mind. How was that possible? Was it a coincidence or had I met her in my life as Greg? Was it possible that on one of his many business trips, Greg had come to Havasu without Hilary knowing? While here, did he see Christy and insert her into his imaginary life?

Suddenly, I realized something. I wasn't sure exactly when it had happened, but I now knew that I was Greg. I had to be. There wasn't any other option. Brad's family didn't exist. I'd proved that in Denver. My house, dog, and handyman business didn't exist. I'd proved that here in Havasu.

Knowing that I was Greg did not change the fact that I still thought of myself as Brad. I preferred Brad's imaginary life and his outlook on life much better than Greg's real life. If I had my way, I was going to live my life as Brad Jones.

I stood up and walked to the window. Right then and there, I made a decision. If Christy didn't show up, I would go to New York and begin making plans for a different life. I hoped it wouldn't take long to resolve issues and get what I needed to set out on my own so I could leave New York for good.

I fluffed the pillows against the headboard, sat against them on the bed and turned on the TV, dividing my attention between channel surfing and the window.

I was jolted out of a deep nap in the late afternoon from the sounds of screaming and yelling in the parking lot. When I looked out, a young couple was arguing next to an SUV. I got the feeling they had been at it for a while. They were taking things out of the SUV, yelling, and cussing at each other at the same time.

Out of the corner of my eye, I saw a red car turn into the parking lot. My head shot around so fast, I almost got whiplash. Unfortunately, I shouldn't have gotten my hopes up. It wasn't Christy.

It was getting close to dinner time and I was getting hungry. I didn't want to leave the room, since I'd told Christy I would be here for two more days. I couldn't bear the thought I would be gone and she'd show up. Would she stick around? Would she leave and come back later? Would she leave and never come back?

Paranoid about missing her if she came by, I thought about my options. What sounded good to eat? I found myself suddenly craving pizza. I decided to call Pizza Hut, order a pizza, and have it delivered. Problem solved.

I ate my dinner while watching TV. I told myself that I accepted the fact that Christy probably wasn't going to show up, but deep in my heart, I hoped beyond hope to see her again.

# Chapter 26

Lake Havasu City, AZ

Christy sat on the couch in her apartment with the TV playing, but she was having a hard time paying attention to it.

She couldn't explain it, but she had become more and more obsessed with the man she'd encountered at Del Taco earlier today. Despite her best efforts, she'd been thinking of him constantly as the day wore on.

*Brad Jones, what is it about you that's so intriguing to me?* Other than the obvious, of course. *He's good-looking with his light brown hair and blue-green eyes. He also has a nice body.* That crazy story about her being in a relationship with him and then getting in a car wreck and ending up in a coma was pretty off-the-wall. In other ways though, he seemed like an honest, upright guy.

*It's like, on some deeper level, I know him. But that's ridiculous,* she'd thought multiple times throughout the day. *I've never seen or heard of him before today.*

She got up and walked into the kitchen for a drink. As she poured herself a glass of ice tea, a memory suddenly flashed into her mind.

A few years ago, she'd gone to Black Bear Diner for breakfast. She'd been craving their Belgium waffles and, unable to find someone to go with her, she went on her own. The place was packed, busier than normal with a long waiting list to be seated. Even the counter seats had a waiting list. She'd decided to forego the waffles until another day.

On her way out, a good-looking guy in a business suit stopped her and asked why she was leaving so soon. When she told him she didn't want to wait an hour for breakfast, he said he was alone and offered to share his table. At that moment, his name was called. On impulse, she decided to stay and sit with him. After all, he seemed like an interesting person, there was a large crowd around, and she could get her waffle fix.

It turned out to be an enjoyable experience. They communicated easily and found many topics they both shared. In fact, they sat at their table and talked for over two hours. After the first hour, the restaurant staff became angry and a little rude about them staying so long while the place was so busy. The man excused himself to go to the restroom and when he came back, the staff bent over backwards to accommodate them. She wondered at the time if he had bribed them. Now, as she thought back on it, she was pretty sure he had.

Her memory about the conversations they had at the encounter was fuzzy, but the more she pictured the guy in her mind, the more she thought he might be Brad. The guy at the diner dressed like a businessman in slacks, a dress shirt, and a jacket. Brad seemed natural in his jeans and T-shirt. Both men, however, were built about the same with the same hair and eye-color. The more she thought about it, the more she felt sure Brad and that guy were the same person. And it gave a clue to how she got inserted into his make-believe life.

She pulled out the phone book, set it on the kitchen counter, and opened the book to the M's. The Motel 6 ad stood out, tempting her to call the number and ask for Room 132.

Feeling a little nervous, she dialed all but the last

number and paused with her finger poised over the phone's screen. Her finger lowered, touching the final number. She put the phone to her ear.

"Thank you for calling Motel 6. How may I help you?"

"Um . . . sorry, wrong number." She ended the call and set the phone down a little too hard on the table. "Oh, boy, what's wrong with me? Why am I so infatuated with this guy? It's not like I'm hard up for a date or anything."

She walked into the living room and shut off the TV. Pacing from room to room, she grew more frustrated by the minute.

During the restaurant encounter with the businessman, he had told her he was only in town for the day. She'd forgotten how disappointed she'd been at the time. She would have liked to have gotten to know him better. Eventually, she'd put him out of her mind. Now, Brad was here, offering her . . . what? She had no idea what to think about the whole situation.

She needed help. She picked up the phone and dialed Trina's number. "Trina, you free for a few hours? I need some advice before I do something really stupid."

"Yeah, sure. What's wrong? You sound stressed."

"I'll explain over dinner."

"Where do you want to go?"

"Pizza Hut. I can't explain it, but I'm craving Pizza Hut pizza tonight. Half-hour?"

"See you there."

As Christy got ready to go, she thought about the strange relationship she had with her mom, Trina. Trina had run off with a biker when Christy was five and lived a biker's life for many years. Her dad remarried. Christy's stepmom raised her like her own daughter. Trina made only occasional contacts throughout Christy's school years. Then, six years ago, Trina showed up in Lake Havasu. After many long talks, arguments, and heartfelt confessions, Christy and Trina decided to start over . . . as friends. Christy couldn't accept Trina as a *mother*. And Trina agreed to that.

Their relationship took a path neither one expected when they became best friends. Now, they rarely mentioned or thought of themselves as mother and daughter. But every now and then, one or the other just couldn't resist getting in a little dig, reminding both that they were more than just friends.

\* \* \*

The smell of pizza dough, tomato sauce, and other delicious toppings greeted Christy when she opened the door to Pizza Hut. Trina, a thin woman in a frilly blouse and long gathered skirt, was waiting on a bench just inside the door. Trina's grey wig was full of uncontrollable curls that she had tied up on the top of her head. Christy never knew which role her mother would play: sometimes the frail older woman and sometimes the hard biker. Tonight it was the frail woman.

The restaurant was busy, but there were a few booths available. The hostess immediately led them past the families, couples, and friends enjoying their dinners. She stopped at a booth and gestured for them to sit down. "Your waitress will be with you in a minute. Enjoy your meal." She put two menus on the table and walked away.

Christy slid onto the plastic red seat on one side of the table while Trina took the other side. Once they were both settled, Trina asked with anticipation, "So, girlfriend, what's got you so riled up tonight?"

"Whoa, not so fast. I'd like to order our food . . . or at least something to drink before I get into it."

"Okay," Trina muttered. "I'm just so curious. I can

hardly wait to hear about it."

After the waitress took their order and left, Christy said, "Okay, you ready?"

Trina nodded.

"I had a strange encounter with a man earlier today."

Trina wiggled her eyebrows and leaned forward. "Oh, do tell."

Christy waved her hand in a gesture of rebuke. "Not that kind of encounter. But it was strange. Since I saw him, I've become obsessed. I find myself thinking about him all the time. I almost called his motel room three or four times today."

"Wow, this sounds interesting. Start from the beginning and tell me everything." Trina sat back and listened intently as Christy told her story.

The food arrived just as Christy finished explaining Brad's approach to her at Del Taco. After taking a bite of pizza, Christy asked, "So, am I crazy for wanting to call him or what?"

"Yes, you are," Trina said, sitting up straight and speaking frankly. "He sounds like a nutcase. Probably escaped from a mental hospital somewhere." She eyed Christy seriously.

Christy shrugged, swallowing the bite. "You could be right. And yet . . . I don't think so."

Trina took a huge bite of hot pizza, then grabbed a napkin to wipe the dripping sauce from her fingers.

While Trina was busy eating, Christy interjected, "You know how you are always telling me to follow my gut instinct?"

"Yeah," Trina mumbled around another big mouthful. "Why do I think I'm not going to like what you say next?"

"I really feel like I need to talk to him. The more I think about it, the more I'm convinced he's telling me the truth. And not only that. Remember a couple of years ago when I met that guy in Black Bear Diner? You know, the one I spent almost three hours talking to?"

Trina's brows raised in immediate recollection. "Do I remember that?" she blurted. "How could I forget? You talked about him for weeks. I remember thinking he must have been a hell of a man to affect you so deeply in such a short time."

"Well, I'm pretty sure Brad, the guy I met today, is the same guy. When he mentioned the name Greg Nordmeyer, it sounded familiar. The more I think about it, I'm positive that was the name of the guy I met in the Black Bear Diner."

"And here we go again." Trina took a deep breath and assumed her typical hard-nosed devil's-advocate role. "Okay . . . say he's telling you the truth. Why would that matter to you? He claims he was in a coma and made up a fake life with you as his girlfriend. Do *you* need to make that life come true?"

"No, of course not," Christy said, growing a little irritated at Trina's resistance. She had hoped for more support. "But it does sound intriguing. It's just that . . . I have a funny feeling I need to talk to him. Even if it's just to help him readjust to his life. He seems confused. Maybe talking to him will help convince him he's Greg, not Brad."

Trina sighed in frustration. "I don't like this."

"He was a gentleman as Greg. I don't see how he would have completely changed his personality, even if he changed his name."

"My god, he was in a coma. Comas change people. I knew a young man who wound up in a coma after a brain injury. He didn't come out of it for months. And when he did, he was never the same again. He, too, couldn't remember who he was for a while. Slowly, he regained some of his memories, but he was never able to function like he had before. Never able to go back to the workplace and make a living. You should be careful that Brad or Greg or whoever he is, is not unstable now, especially since he can't remember his other life. Who knows what else he made up as Brad? He could be dangerous."

Christy wiped her mouth with a napkin. "Even if he can't remember who he is, he comes across to me as stable. There's nothing about him that tells me he is dangerous."

Trina shook her head. "Okay, but I'm warning you, if he kills you and dismembers your body, don't come running to me."

Christy laughed. "If he does that I won't be running to anybody."

"You want me to go with you. Act as your backup?"

"*No!*" she barked. *I don't want Trina there watching my every move. She'd be right in the middle of everything and probably mess the whole thing up.*

"You sure. I don't mind."

"I'll be fine," Christy insisted. "Besides, I'm not going into his room or anything. I'm going to make him meet me in a public place tomorrow during my lunch break. It'll be sunny outside with lots of people around. I'm not stupid, you know."

"I know, sweetie. You know how I worry about you."

"Yeah. I love you, too, Mom. I appreciate your concern and your willingness to listen to me and give me your insights. But, as we both know, I make my own choices in the end."

Trina smiled and picked up the check as the waitress dropped it on the table.

# Chapter 27

## Lake Havasu City, AZ

I was up bright and early the next day. I clung to the hope that Christy would show up today. It meant I would have to be confined to the motel room all day, but if that's what it took, that's what I would do.

I debated about calling Hilary. I felt it was only courteous to let her know I would be staying a few days longer than I'd told her on Friday morning, but I wasn't looking forward to telling her why. After our heated conversation that morning, I figured she might suspect I would not be wanting to come back to New York right away and not be concerned about it. In the end, I decided against calling her.

After taking a quick shower, I called IHOP and arranged for a carryout breakfast. It was still early enough that Christy probably wouldn't show up until later. Besides, it was Monday. If she had a job, she'd have to work around her schedule.

I hurried to IHOP and back. A ham and cheese omelet with hash browns, white toast, strawberry jam, and orange juice hit the spot. When I finished eating, I looked outside and saw a trash can sitting three doors down the sidewalk. As I shoved my breakfast trash into the container, I heard a phone ring. I looked back at my open door. It was the phone in my room!

A family with three kids and lots of luggage chose that moment to come out of a room between me and my phone. They blocked the whole sidewalk. Darting between two cars, I ran into the parking lot, hurried behind three cars, and turned toward my room. I sprinted for the door, ignoring the strange looks from the family. I used the bed to stop my forward momentum and grabbed the phone from the bedside stand.

"Hello?" I said breathlessly.

"Brad?" It was a woman, but not Christy. And yet, other than Christy and Hilary, nobody knew I was here at the motel.

"Yes, this is Brad. Who's this?"

"You sound winded. Do you have a breathing problem?"

"No, I ran to catch the phone before you hung up."

"Well, okay. My name is Trina. I'm a friend of someone you met yesterday."

Chills ran down my arms. She had to be calling for Christy. "Yes," I said, trying to keep my voice steady and stop my heart from pounding.

"I'm sure you know who I'm talking about, don't you?"

"Yes I do. Why the subterfuge?" I started to sweat. Did Christy put her up to this to tell me she wouldn't see me?

"She's at work and couldn't call, so she asked me if I would call and give you a message. Personally, I think this whole thing feels like a story from the Twilight Zone."

"I have to agree," I said. "I take it she's told you about me?"

"Yes. And I told her she was crazy for having anything to do with you. She wants to meet up with you today."

I did a fist pump in the air. *Awesome, she wants to see*

*me.*

She continued in a hard, unfriendly voice. "I want you to know that she's got a lot of friends who would think nothing of messing you up really bad if you hurt her in any way. Do I make myself clear?"

The threat came through loud and clear. "Crystal clear. I promise you, I'm not out to hurt her. In fact, if you want to be there when we meet, that's fine with me."

"I wanted to be there with her, but it is her wish that it just be the two of you. Personally, I think she's nuts."

"Don't worry. I'd be happy to meet her in a public place with lots of people around."

"Good, because that's exactly what is going to happen. During her lunch break at high noon, be at the stage under the London Bridge. You know where that is?"

"Yes, I do. Tell her I'll be there."

"With bells on?" she said sarcastically.

"No, with love in my heart."

"You're so full of crap, I can smell you from here. I'm warning you, if you hurt her you won't be able to run far enough to hide. I will find you." The phone clicked as the call disconnected.

If the situation was reversed, I'd probably feel the same way as Trina. In a way, I was glad Christy had such a good friend. I was determined to prove to Trina that I was no threat to Christy.

I looked at the clock. Three long grueling hours until noon.

*     *     *

Thirty minutes early, I sat under the London Bridge on the open stage. I didn't have anything else to do but wait. At least here, I could watch people come and go instead of sitting alone in my motel room.

I picked up a brochure about the area. In 1967, the London Bridge had been bought, dismantled, and brought to Lake Havasu where it now spanned the Bridgewater Channel. Under the bridge, a three-foot-high, forty-by-forty concrete stage had been built for outdoor bands and concerts. Souvenir shops, restaurants, and boat and paddle-board rentals lined the cement walking path, which ran along the edge of the channel for about a half-mile to the north and two miles south to Rotary Park.

Right at noon, I saw Christy enter the walking path from the main parking lot. I stood up, but I didn't approach her. I felt it was the smart thing to do.

She smiled at me as she walked toward me.

"Hi," I said.

"Hi, yourself."

"So . . . ." I scanned the area. "You want to sit here on the stage, go in the burger joint, or what?"

"For now, this is fine." She sat on the edge of the stage.

Not wanting to crowd her, I sat down about two feet away.

She looked great in a pair of dark slacks and a light-blue button-up, long-sleeved shirt over a white tank top. Seeing the sandals on her feet convinced me she wasn't planning on running away from me. Other than her longer, lighter-colored hair, she looked exactly like my memories told me she should.

"Okay, I'm here," she said, folding her arms over her chest. "Talk."

I told her everything I remembered as Brad from the time I'd met her years ago, right up to the funny feelings, the accident, waking from the coma, and living with Hilary. She stopped me a few times to clarify certain things, but for the most part, she just let me talk. I'd told a lot of people the whole story, but listening to myself tell it to the woman I shared the experience with as Brad seemed strange. She hadn't actually been there. It must have been strange for her, too, to have heard such a detailed life with me.

When I finished, she said, "So, in your heart, who do you think you are?"

"Brad Jones. No doubt in my mind."

"Who do you think you used to be?"

Truth time. "Greg Nordmeyer."

"But not anymore?"

"No."

"So, as far as you're concerned, you don't have a wife and three kids waiting for you in New York?"

I pictured Hilary sitting every morning at the breakfast table with her bagel and jam. "No, I don't."

"She still thinks you're her husband and the father of her children, doesn't she?"

"Yes."

"What are you going to do about that?"

"Whatever I need to do."

She got up and paced about ten feet away, then turned and looked at me. "I believe you."

"You do?" I blurted in shock.

"Yes." She reached into her back pocket and pulled out a business card. Coming toward me, she handed it to me. "I have to go back to work soon, so before I forget, I want to give you my number. Maybe we can get together again before you leave."

"Thanks." I was thrilled that she was interested enough to let me call her. I pulled out my wallet and stuck the card in it.

"I have to tell you," she went on, pacing another few feet away. "When I saw you yesterday, I thought you looked familiar. I'm positive we met a couple of years ago at a restaurant."

"What do you mean?"

"You were in a business suit and invited me to have breakfast with you. The restaurant was packed and I was alone and would have had to wait an hour to eat. You were kind enough to share your table with me."

*Aha! Greg had come to Havasu. Hilary didn't know about it.* Things were starting to fall into place. "And?"

"And . . . I'm about to do something very, very foolish." She came toward me.

On impulse, I stood up.

She took both my hands in hers. "I know I'm moving into this really fast," she said, "and I'm not sure where it's going to end up. But I need to find out. I have this *funny feeling* we are destined to be together. I can't explain it. I do know that I can't get you off my mind. I couldn't get Greg off my mind, either, for a long time. I know this sounds crazy, seeing as how we just met yesterday, but I think the life you described that we had together sounds beautiful."

Relief flooded over me. I had been afraid she would think I was insane and run away as fast as she could. Now, it looked like I had a chance to have her love in my life. "You don't know how happy I am to hear you say that."

She smiled, then asked sheepishly, "Will you give me a kiss?"

I would have loved to grab her and hold her passionately in my arms, but something told me to act appropriately in this public place.

She gently pulled me to her and closed her eyes as I gave her a tender kiss on the lips.

When I pulled back, she smiled. Her eyes beamed. "That was perfect. Thank you."

A loud voice interrupted our reverie. "That's enough. You'll regret it if you go any further." A thin woman stood about five feet away. Of average height, she wore faded jeans with a hole in one knee, a biker vest over a black T-shirt, and lace-up combat boots. Her short black hair was spiked. Overall, she looked hard and mean. Not someone I would want to mess with.

Christy turned toward the woman and said irritably, "Trina! What are you doing here?"

"Making sure you're safe."

"I told you I would be okay. There are plenty of people here. And, as you can see, I don't need to be rescued. I'm fine."

"Looks to me like he's moving a little too fast. You don't know what might be on his mind." Trina looked around, "And the only one running to help you is me."

I stepped up next to Christy and put my arm around her waist. "Trina, I'm not going to hurt her, I promise. I have a few things to take care of in New York." I glanced at Christy. "Then everything will be good again."

Christy started to ask me a question, but I cut her off. "I'll explain over dinner tonight, okay?"

Trina shook her head. "Christy, please, don't fall for his fairytale story. Think about it for a day or two. At least Google him and make sure he's not one of those men who prey on innocent women. You owe it to me and your friends to take your time with this. You don't know anything about him. He could have a split personality. He could be a mass murderer on a killing spree. Don't rush into something that could destroy your life. Please?"

Christy seemed to waver about what to do. Turning her back on Trina, she rolled her eyes, as if to say to me that she had to take care of this woman first. She stepped away from me and said, "Brad, maybe I am moving a little too fast. Give me some time to think about it. I'm not sure about dinner tonight." She looked at her watch. "Right now, I have to get back to work."

"Um, sure," I mumbled, devastated at the sudden turn of events.

Trina grabbed Christy's arm and turned her toward the parking lot.

Clearly annoyed, Christy shook her arm free.

I could hear them talking in an argumentative tone, but the words were too faint for me to make out what they were saying.

Just before they disappeared, Christy turned and looked at me.

I waved.

She nodded without returning the wave. Was she walking out of my life . . . again?

# Chapter 28

Lake Havasu City, AZ

$B$ack in my room, I fell onto the bed and stared at the ceiling. My emotions were going up and down faster than a bride's nightie on her wedding night.

Beautiful, touching moments floated through my mind: Christy taking my hands, asking me to kiss her, kissing her sweet lips, looking into her twinkling eyes. These emotions were interrupted with confusion and fear, like Christy agreeing with Trina that she needed time to think about us, not committing to having dinner with me, walking away without waving. I didn't know what to think.

I pulled Christy's card out of my pocket and held it like a treasure. She had offered her number without me asking. That had to say something. But then again, that was before Trina showed up. Should I call her now or not? I wasn't sure.

I spent a good deal of time considering Greg's life and the little bit of it I had seen when I had gone home with Hilary. No matter what would happen with Christy, I already had made up my mind that I wasn't going to live in White Plains, with or without Hilary.

I may have been Greg before the accident, but now I was Brad, and Brad was going to do what Brad wanted to do. I'm sure I'd known for some time that I wouldn't be living in New York. Maybe when I'd been sitting in that coffee shop in Denver. Why else would I have driven to Havasu on such impulse? What had made me think that, after failing to find my parents, daughter, and sister, I would find anyone in Havasu who would know me? Maybe I was looking for a new home.

Tired from the stress of the emotional ups and downs, I closed my eyes and tried to sleep. I dosed fitfully for an hour, got up and turned on the TV, shut it off when finding nothing that would hold my attention, and opened my door. Stepping outside, I looked out over the parking lot, which was just starting to fill up with cars coming in for the afternoon reservations.

By now it was close to 3:00 p.m. I hadn't eaten since breakfast, but I wasn't that hungry. I grabbed a candy bar in the vending machine and sat on the bed in my room while I ate it.

Hilary and Christy kept weaving through my mind like broken records. They were the only two women in my life at the moment, and both held significant importance in their own ways.

I stood up, shaking myself. *I have to get my mind off all this.* I thought about taking a walk, since the London Bridge shops and Rotary Park were in a decent walking distance. First though, I worried that Christy might call while I was gone. *Do I dare call her, especially so soon?* I figured she was still at work right now and I didn't want her to get in trouble for getting phone calls while she was on the job. I didn't even know what she did for a living.

Feeling antsy and wanting to get my body moving, I decided to take a chance. I picked up the motel phone and dialed the cell phone number on Christy's card. I was hoping she wouldn't answer, and luckily, she didn't. In fact, her phone didn't even ring. It went straight to voice mail.

"Hi, Christy. It's me, Brad . . . I'm thinking of going for a walk and was worried you might call the room and . . . " *Crap, I'm messing this up so bad.* "Well, anyway, I . . . if you call and I don't answer, leave a message and I'll call you back."

I hung up and stared at the phone. Why had I used the motel phone instead of my cell phone? And why hadn't I given her my cell number? *What an idiot,* I thought as I grabbed my room key and cell phone from the table by the window. Feeling like a fool, I stood by the door a few minutes, trying to decide if I should call her back or not. I opted to not make a further fool of myself and left for the walk.

*   *   *

When I got back to the motel, I felt tired but refreshed. I had burned off enough energy that my mind had cleared somewhat. I felt an urge to get back to New York and take care of things, once and for all.

Unfortunately, that meant it was time to call Hilary. I had no idea how to arrange for a private flight back to New York. I could fly commercial out of Vegas, but I still wasn't comfortable using Greg's credit cards and I didn't know if I had enough cash left to cover a flight.

*Hilary.* That whole situation was a mess. I had thought quite a bit about what I was going to tell her the next time I talked to her. Well . . . in reality, I'd already known for some time what I was going to tell her. I just needed to figure out how to explain to a woman that I didn't know or love that I wanted a divorce. A woman whose whole life revolved around her husband's money and her social status. I certainly didn't want to get into it on the phone. Something like that needed to be discussed in person.

I took a deep breath and prepared myself for what I expected to be an unpleasant phone call. She'd hung up on me after that one call I'd made to her last Friday, so I wasn't even sure she would talk to me.

Knowing I had to get on with it, I pulled out my phone, held down number one, and put the phone to my ear while it did its thing.

"Yes, Gregory?" Hilary answered coldly.

"Yeah, um . . . I'm ready to come back. Do you want me to fly commercial or can you arrange a private flight?"

"Let me see what I can do. I'll call you back."

I paced the floor while I waited, wondering if I was doing the right thing by leaving.

Fifteen minutes later she called back. "Hertz doesn't have an office in Lake Havasu, so you need to drive to Las Vegas to drop off the rental car. Your flight leaves Las Vegas at eight a.m. tomorrow morning. Can you be there by then?"

"Yes. I'll leave here early."

"I'll have the limo meet you at the airport."

"Okay."

She hung up.

Yes, I think she was still angry about our last conversation, or maybe she was mad that I hadn't called her until now. *Oh well. She's going to be even angrier when I tell her I want a divorce.*

I didn't know where I stood with Christy, but I felt it would be better to take care of things in New York before we got involved. For sure, I was going to return from New York as soon as possible to find out whether or not we could make a life together.

I dialed Christy's number. Once again, it went straight to voice mail. "Hi, Christy. It's Brad. Listen, I'm going to cancel my dinner invitation tonight. You need time to think about this whole thing, and I have some things I have to do. I'm going back to New York tomorrow. I don't know how long I'll be gone, perhaps a couple of weeks, maybe a month. I will definitely be back. If you want to call me, I would like that." I gave her my cell phone number and hung up.

The ball was now in her court. Would she play or would she concede the game and walk away?

As for me, I wanted to get on with my own life and put the troublesome things behind me.

# Chapter 29

## White Plains, NY

The flight back to New York took six hours. I left Vegas at 8:00 a.m. and arrived at 2:00 p.m. Arizona time. With the time change, the plane touched down at 5:00 p.m. As we taxied off the runway, I was startled by my cell phone ringing.

"Hello?"

"Brad? It's me, Christy."

I was excited, nervous, and scared all at the same time. "It's good to hear from you . . . How are you doing?"

"Good . . . I just got off work . . . I'm walking out to my car. How are you?"

"I'm good . . . my plane just landed. We're taxiing to the terminal now."

There was a long pause. Suddenly, I had a déjà vu moment from junior high when I had called my girlfriend. Like now, back then neither one of us knew quite what to say.

My discomfort got even worse when I saw Hilary step out of a limo. I didn't want to cut the phone call with Christy short, but I couldn't very well talk to her with Hilary standing next to me.

"Would it be better if we talked later?" Christy finally said. "I know you'll have to get off the plane and get your luggage and everything."

Whew, she gave me an out. "Yeah, that would be great. I'll call you when I get settled in, and . . . "

"And you have some free time alone," she finished for me, probably suspecting Hilary was going to be hanging around.

"Yeah . . . give me an hour or two and I'll call you back, okay?"

"Sounds good."

I started to pull the phone from my ear when I heard, "And Brad?"

Hurriedly, I put the phone back to my ear. "Yeah?"

"I'm looking forward to talking to you."

"I'm looking forward to talking to you, too. Bye."

As I put my phone away, I realized this was the only call that had come in during the entire time I had the phone. I checked to see what contacts had been listed. Only Hilary's cell phone and home phone. For the first time, I realized that by giving me this phone, Hilary had kept me from having to deal with any of the family members or business calls that might have haunted Greg. She had told me that very thing when she had given me the phone, so I guess I had to be thankful for that. My trip across the country hadn't been muddied by any interruptions from unwanted demands in New York.

I put the phone away when the pilot announced our arrival at the terminal.

Grabbing my overnight bag, sleeping bag, and items I'd bought on my trip to Havasu, I leaned into the cockpit and thanked the pilot for the flight. I slowly walked down the stairs to the tarmac. Even though I wasn't exerting myself, my breaths grew short and butterflies raged in my stomach. I was more nervous about meeting face to face with Hilary than dealing with any other event that had taken place since I'd awakened in the nursing home.

Hilary leaned against the limo with her arms folded.

As I got closer, she pushed herself off the car. "How was the flight?"

"Good." Being uneasy, I was glad she didn't try to give me a hug or a kiss.

Martin took my bags and put them in the trunk.

Hilary glanced at the sleeping bag with disgust but didn't say anything about it. She was probably wondering if I was the only one who had slept in it.

The trip to the house was awkward, to say the least. What little conversation we had was stilted and rife with pauses. Most of the time, I looked out the window and wished this was all over.

* * *

When we got to the house, Hilary went into the kitchen, and I went upstairs to the guest room to put my stuff away. I threw it on the bed. Before opening my overnight bag, Hilary called from downstairs, "Gregory, could we talk?"

I froze in place. *Show time.* I dreaded the coming conversation, but I had to face up to it eventually. I walked down the stairs slowly, each step filled with trepidation.

Hilary sat at the kitchen table. A bottle of wine and a half-empty glass sat in front of her. Her movements were stiff and jerky. Her eyes were cold and mean. An aura of tension surrounded her, increasing my own uneasiness.

I thought about grabbing something to drink. I didn't like wine and I'd never seen beer in the fridge. I wasn't sure alcohol was a good thing to indulge in, anyway, not while having the type of conversation we were about to face. Deciding I didn't want anything, I pulled out a chair and sat down. When she didn't say anything, I started. "I guess you're curious about my trip."

"Yes, I am." She took a big sip of wine, almost emptying the glass.

There was no sense in putting it off. I dived right into the story. "As you know, Denver was a bust. I didn't find any sign of my parents, my sister, or my daughter."

"And what about Havasu?" She poured more wine. "Did you find anyone there you knew?"

I knew she was more interested in what I'd found in Havasu than anything else. Havasu held the biggest threat to her. Namely Christy. And yet, that was one thing I wasn't ready to discuss. If I told her about Christy, she'd freak out. She'd probably kick me out of the house immediately, and I needed to take care of a few things first and make arrangements for leaving New York. I didn't have a lot of options at the moment to just walk out of the house with nothing. Plus, I wanted to do things on my own terms and in my own time.

"No, I didn't." Technically, it wasn't a lie. Brad didn't know *Christy*. He knew *Chrissy*. Greg had met Christy years ago, but Brad only met her a few days ago at Del Taco. Even though she looked almost exactly like the Chrissy in my mind, she was a different person. She even had a different name.

The tension didn't leave Hilary's face, and her eyes remained cold and mean. "Did the town or anything in Arizona look familiar?"

I explained how some things, like my house, client houses, and streets looked the same. And how I'd known exactly where some of them were located. I was right about the Sunday swap meet. On the other hand, a lot of things were not how I remembered them. "All in all, the trip left me more confused than ever."

"What do you mean?" She took a small sip of wine. Getting away from the *girlfriend* subject seemed to slow the consumption of wine considerably.

"Well . . . I'm pretty much convinced I'm Greg. But if

I am, how would I know Havasu so well?"

She pursed her lips and glared at me. "I don't know. I certainly can't explain it. You did a lot of traveling. Maybe you went there and didn't tell me about it. . . . In fact, most of the time," she added with accusation, "you didn't tell me where you were going. I trusted it was always on business."

Greg went to Havasu at least once, according to Christy, and it probably wasn't on business. Maybe there were a lot of off-the-business-path places he visited and didn't tell Hilary. Maybe traveling was his only form of freedom.

"Well, it doesn't matter now," she said in an authoritarian manner as she stood up. "You are home. We can put it all behind us and get my life . . . *our* lives back." She walked a little tipsy out of the room.

I chuckled to myself when she started to say *her life*. That's what all of this had been about anyway. Even her offering of the trip to Denver had been her way to convince me I was Greg so that she could get on with her life. Poor Hilary. It wasn't going to be that easy for her to put it behind her. If she only knew what the next few days were going to bring.

I was glad she left the room. Being exhausted from the trip and having jetlag, I feared I might slip and say something about Christy. Also, it didn't seem to be the appropriate time to bring up the divorce issue. Hilary wasn't in a condition to be reasoned with, not that she ever would be.

I looked at the clock. It was dinner time. I noticed Stella wasn't in the kitchen. I wondered if Hilary called off dinner because she didn't want to sit across from me.

I found some meat and cheese slices in the fridge, made a sandwich, and took it up to my room.

Anxious to get back to Christy, I dialed her number. Again, it went straight to voice mail. I wondered if she was screening her calls or if she legitimately didn't hear the phone ring. I left a short message and hung up. I couldn't wait to get back to Arizona where I could be with her all the time.

# Chapter 30

## Lake Havasu City, AZ

Christy had aimlessly walked around the parking lot while she'd talked to Brad on the phone. Feeling hopeful about what the future with Brad might bring, she hung up and headed for her car with a light step.

She noticed two young men in baggy pants and tight-fitting tank-tops leaning against the trunk of a white, four-door car with black tinted windows and two stickers in the back window. The car had been modified by lowering the suspension and was parked on the opposite side of the aisle.

As she got closer to her car, the two men pushed off the car trunk and started walking toward her. Feeling uneasy, she took her keys out of her purse and hoped to get to the car before they reached her.

The men sped up, causing Christy's heart to race in fear. Walking faster, she looked around for someone who could help her. Although the parking lot was full of cars, not a single person was in sight.

Smiling, the two men stopped twenty feet from her car. One of them held out his hand and gave a half-bow, as if saying, "Sorry we scared you. Go ahead and get in your car." They looked to be in their late teens, maybe early twenties. One wore a red-and-white ball cap. The other wore a black-and-red one. The brims of both hats faced backwards.

Thinking she'd come to the wrong conclusion about them, she continued walking, wishing she had a remote-control key fob. While keeping an eye on the men, she clumsily tried sticking the key in the key hole. When the lock turned, the two men rushed toward her.

She let out a startled scream. Yanking the key from the lock, she jerked the door open.

Before she got halfway into the car, one of the men grabbed her by the arm and pulled her out. He slammed her chest against the back door. Gripping her upper arms with both hands, he leaned his body against hers so she couldn't move.

Panicking about what they were going to do, she turned her head and saw the second man slowly pull a gun out of the front pocket of his baggy pants. She took a deep breath to scream, but the hand holding her right arm moved to her throat and squeezed, effectively silencing her.

"Calm down, lady. We aren't going to hurt you. At least not today." His breath was sour, as if he'd hadn't brushed his teeth in years. "We've got a message for you. If I let you go, do you promise not to yell or try to run away?"

With a gun involved, she'd be stupid to argue or scream. She could be shot before anyone could get to her. Trying to outrun a bullet would be futile. She nodded her head in agreement.

The man removed his hand from her throat and turned her around to face him. He kept one hand on her shoulder as a reminder not to run.

"What do you want? Money? Take it," she said, holding out her purse.

The man with the gun chuckled. "That's funny, Dave. She thinks this is a robbery."

Dave shoved the other man's shoulder, almost

knocking him down. "Idiot, don't use our real names."

"Oh, yeah. Sorry, Dave." He cringed. "Sorry."

Dave turned back to Christy. "We have a message for you. That's all." Seeming to be satisfied that she wasn't going to scream or run away, he took two steps backwards and stood next to the man with the gun.

Christy quickly scanned the parking lot for people. No luck. She hoped the men were right about not hurting her. "What's the message?"

The man with the gun said, "A certain person, who shall remain ominous—"

His partner shot a dirty look at him. "It's *anonymous*, you idiot."

"Oh, right. This certain person, who shall remain anonymous, for fear of being incapacitated—"

Dave shook his head. "It's *implicated*, Mark, not incapacitated."

"I thought we weren't using our real names," Mark whined.

"*Shit*," Dave blurted. "You're screwing it up and getting me flustered. I'm taking over."

"Sure, Dave, whatever."

Even in her fear, Christy felt like laughing. These two were a joke. But they still had a gun on her.

Dave said, "It seems as though you've been seeing the husband of a certain person who lives in a big town back east. She never wants you to see him again. Her exact words: 'Make sure Christy never contacts Gregory again.' If you do," he nodded at Mark, "we'll come back and bad things will happen to you. Or to your friends or your family. You understand?"

*Oh, my god, this is about Brad.* Christy nodded to appease them.

"Yeah," Mark chimed in, weaving the gun around in erratic motions as he talked. "We know your mom lives here in Havasu. Your sister and her family live here, too, on Acoma Boulevard. We know where the kids go to school. We have the addresses of some of your friends here in town. You better stay away or we'll come back and fu—"

A loud bang startled Christy.

Mark looked at the gun and held it out by two fingers, like it was a dangerous animal about to bite him. Smoke slowly drifted out of the muzzle.

"Holy shit, Mark," Dave blurted. "We weren't supposed to use the gun. What if you would have shot her?" He spun around to see if anyone might have heard the shot.

A sharp pain flared in the upper left side of Christy's chest. She looked down and saw a a hole in her white blouse. A red stain slowly spread out from the hole, moving downward. At this point, everything started moving in slow motion.

She heard Mark whimper, "I didn't mean for it to go off. It did it by itself, I promise. Here, take it."

"I don't want it. It's got your fingerprints on it."

Blood seeped out from between Christy's fingers and trickled down her arm. "Hey . . . guys. A little help here?"

Dave and Mark stopped talking. Their eyes widened at the sight of the blood drenching Christy's side. They shot a look at each other and took off running toward their car.

Behind Christy, another car turned the corner in the parking lot and moved toward her. She took two stumbling steps into the path of the car and collapsed to the ground. Tires screeched to a stop. A car door opened and closed. Hurried footsteps approached as blackness crept into to corners of her mind, threatening to take control.

In the distance, she heard a car burning rubber as it headed out of the parking lot.

"You okay?" a woman asked, touching her lightly on the back. She rolled Christy over a little and gasped. "Oh, my god. You've been shot."

*Brad. I just met Brad. I don't want to die yet. I want the life he told me about.*

The blackness descended, taking her to a place with no pain, no awareness, no nothing.

# Chapter 31

The next morning, I tried calling Christy again. Her phone went straight to voice mail. I was disappointed and growing frustrated that I couldn't get a hold of her. Maybe she was busy getting ready for work. Maybe she was in the shower. Maybe I was calling at the wrong times and she couldn't answer her phone. I didn't want to think she'd changed her mind about talking with me. At the moment, there was nothing I could do about it. If she didn't call back, I'd try calling again in the afternoon.

I went downstairs to find Hilary. I wandered around the house and found Stella in the laundry room. She had rolled up her sleeves and was putting clothes in the washing machine.

"Excuse me," I said, poking my head around the corner of the door. "Have you seen Hilary today?"

"Yes," she said, brushing a stray strand of dark hair out of her eyes. "She had a few errands to run. She was going to stop at the store on her way home."

Perfect. I was hoping I wouldn't run into her today.

"Would you like some breakfast?"

"No thanks. I'm going out for a while. I'll pick something up."

She shrugged and went back to her laundry.

For the first time, I noticed the tattoos on her arms. *No*

*wonder she always wears long sleeves when Hilary's around.* I figured the tattoos were related to Stella's former gang days.

In the kitchen, I rummaged through drawers until I found a phone book. I took the phone book, a small pad of paper, and a pencil with me to the garage and got in the Mercedes.

I stopped at a McDonalds and ordered two ham-and-egg McMuffins, a hash brown, and a glass of orange juice. With my bag of food, I parked in a secluded parking spot to eat while I searched through the phone book for an attorney. I wrote down the names of six attorneys. Not the ones with the big fancy ads. I noted ones who listed only their names and phone numbers. Hopefully, one of them would be able to see me today. If not, I would look up more numbers.

I got lucky on the third call. A male answered and said he could see me anytime this morning. I liked his friendly and enthusiastic attitude. I told him I would be there in a half-hour or so.

I then looked up motels in the area and punched an address into the GPS. Lucky me. It was only two blocks away. I pulled into the Motel 6 lot and walked into the office. Ten minutes later, I had reserved a room for the next week, paid in cash from the money I still had in my wallet. I would need to come back later to get my key, but at least I had the room reserved. My cash was getting low, but I hoped that would be resolved soon.

The attorney's office was about five miles from the motel, and I made it within the half-hour with a few minutes to spare.

The office was in a drab, run-down three-story building that hadn't had a good cleaning or a paint job in many years. The parking lot was full of pot holes. It had so many cracks in it, I was surprised it was able to hold itself together.

The inside of the building showed no improvement over the outside. The worn, vinyl floor hadn't seen a broom, a mop, or a wax job in years. The chipped, faded yellow paint contrasted sharply with the two still-life paintings of fruit hanging on the walls.

I climbed the stairs to the third floor. A plaque on the door of one of the offices read: *Phillip Stanger, Attorney at Law.*

I turned the knob and pushed the door open. A little bell jingled at the top of the door. Having seen the outside and lobby of the building, I wasn't expecting much and, therefore, I wasn't disappointed.

The reception area consisted of one room, about twenty-by-twenty feet. An old, striped couch that had seen way too much use, sat against the wall on my left. The wall on my right had two floral-print easy chairs that were probably older than I was. A large painting of a tropical beach hung over the two chairs. Two smaller beach scenes hung crookedly on the wall above the couch. I got an urge to straighten them, but I resisted.

It was hard to tell if the carpet was clean or dirty. The brown coloring hid the dirt, but the dark color couldn't hide the wear patterns. A door in the center of the far wall was bordered on each side by fake plants, which sat in the corners.

Judging by the appearance of the office, I expected to see an old, down-on-his-luck attorney. *I just hope he's not a drunk.*

Before I could decide whether or not to knock on the door, it opened and a young man wearing jeans, a dress shirt with no tie, and tennis shoes stepped out. I thought he might be the secretary or an assistant or something.

"Hi," he said, walking toward me. "I'm Phillip Stanger. You must be Brad Jones."

Hiding my surprise, I shook his extended hand. "Nice to meet you, Phillip." Immediately, I liked his open, youthful exuberance.

"I know what you're thinking," he said as he motioned toward the room. "Not a very impressive office for an attorney, right?"

I shrugged my shoulders. "The thought did cross my mind."

"When I was in law school, I decided I wasn't going to work for one of those high-and-mighty law firms." He nodded his head toward the office and started walking in that direction.

I followed him.

"I wanted to make a difference in peoples lives. And not by taking all their hard-earned money. I decided I would operate out of an inexpensive office so I could help people who really needed the help of an attorney."

This was great. It was exactly what I had been looking for. I couldn't believe I'd lucked onto him so fast. I hoped he could handle what I needed him to do.

He sat at a plain and simple wooden desk.

I took a seat on what looked like an old dining room table chair. Two of them sat in front of his desk, while two more were lined up against a wall next to a filing cabinet. A laptop computer, a printer, and a fax machine sat on an old scarred desk in one corner. I glanced around the room. It was clean, but not high-and-mighty clean. A light film of dust covered out-of-the-way surfaces, but the desk and chairs were dust-free.

Sunlight shown through a dirty window. A spider in a web told me it had been a long time since the window had been opened. I took this to mean that Phillip had better things to do than dust and wash windows.

"So, Brad, what can I do for you today?" Placing his hands against the desk, he leaned back in his office chair.

"I hope you have an hour free," I said. "My story is kind of long and complicated."

He grinned. "I'm free for the next three hours."

I launched into my story. I'd only talked for a few minutes when he got out a yellow legal notepad and started writing down notes. His demeanor changed from casual and carefree to serious and intrigued the more I talked. Like everyone else who had heard my story, he interrupted me a few times to clarify a point or to ask a question about something.

When I finished, he said, "Okay . . . so I take it you're not going to live here in New York with Hilary, are you?"

I shook my head.

A big grin crossed his face. "I'll bet you're going to go to Arizona, hook up with Christy, and never look back, aren't you?"

I nodded. "Wouldn't you?"

He chuckled. "So, you'll be wanting me to file divorce papers, right?"

"Among other things." I smiled, confident I'd made a wise decision by choosing Phillip.

# Chapter 32

White Plains, NY

I managed to avoid Hilary until later that afternoon. I was just starting down the stairs with a load of my clothes and personal things when she caught me.

Looking up from the bottom step, she gave me a stern look. "What are you doing?"

"Um, I guess we need to talk."

Frostily, she said, "Yes, I suppose we do." She turned and headed for the kitchen. By the time I got down the stairs, set the stuff to the side, and walked into the kitchen, she had gotten a bottle out of the fridge and was pouring herself a large glass of wine, clear to the brim.

I sat on the opposite side of the table. "Listen, Hilary, I think it's best if I move out for a while." I held up my hand to stave off her rebuttal. "I've already arranged to stay at a motel for the next week. I'll see how I feel about things at that time."

"I see." She took a big sip of wine. "And just what is it you hope to prove with this foolish move?"

I had figured she would fight this and make a big deal out of it. I told myself I had to stay strong, not only for me, but for Christy, too. "I'm hoping I can come to terms with what's happening to me."

"Gregory, do you know how that's going to look if you move out? People are already starting to talk. I don't need this in my life right now."

I stood up and slammed my hand down on the table, startling her so sharply, she spilled a little bit of wine. "For god's sake, woman, don't you understand what I'm going through? All you care about is you, your life, your wellbeing. Well, I've got news for you, I'm leaving and there's not a damn thing you can do about it."

Her eyes narrowed and her lips pinched so tightly they disappeared. "If you think I'm going to sit back and do nothing while you gallivant around with your little girlfriend, you've got another thing coming."

*Ahh ha*! I saw where her mind was going with this. "This has nothing to do with Crissy," I snarled. "This is about me . . . and only me. I need to have some time to figure out what to do next."

She huffed. "Are you threatening divorce?"

"Why? If I did, would it ruin your social standing? Would you lose the memberships at your precious clubs?"

She stood up and got a paper towel. As she wiped up the spilled wine, she said in a cool tone, "You should know, Gregory, I've been in touch with Timothy Medford. He and I have made some contingency plans, just in case something like this happened."

"And Timothy is . . . who?" I asked, holding my arms out, palms turned up.

She smiled a wicked smile. "Our family attorney. You know, the one who handles all the nasty little legal problems that pop up every now and then? You and Timothy went to school together."

"Well, I've talked to an attorney, too," I blurted.

Shock filled her eyes. "Who?" She stammered for a moment. "When did you do that?" Before I could answer, she continued. "Never mind. It doesn't matter. Whoever you are working with can't be as good as Timothy. He's the top attorney in the state. Everyone wants him to handle their cases. We are one of the lucky families to have him on retainer." She laughed viciously. "It's ironic, isn't it?"

I gave her a blank look.

"Timothy always resented you, your wealth, your prestige, your position in life. It came natural to you. He had to work hard to get what he attained. Not to mention the fact that you always insisted on calling him *Timmy*. Believe me, he has no problem taking on this case." She took a sip of wine, watching me closely.

I didn't react, just stood there and looked at her.

She seemed a little disappointed.

I didn't remember *Timmy* any more than I remembered anyone else, and I could care less about him. My attorney was young and resourceful. He had a few tricks up his sleeve that were going to blow Timmy out of the water. "Whatever," I said calmly. "Are we through here? I have things I need to do."

She glared at me. She knew there was nothing she could do. "Go. Have fun. Do whatever. But, Gregory, we will talk again. Tomorrow."

"Why not now? Why not say it all now?"

She poured herself more wine. "You'll see."

It was clear she had something to talk about, but for some reason, wasn't ready. If I wanted to, I could always avoid her tomorrow. I wouldn't be in the house. On second thought, avoiding her might not be the best idea. Any information she was willing to tell me could be possible ammunition Phillip could use against her. I didn't like playing these kind of mind games, but I figured I only had a month at the most. Then I'd be out of here and in Arizona with Christy.

I left Hilary at the table with her wine, collected my stuff, and loaded it into the Mercedes.

As soon as I got into my room at the motel, I tried Christy's number. Again, straight to voice mail.

Now I was getting worried. Why wouldn't she answer her phone? I couldn't imagine why she would keep avoiding me after her friendly call when the plane landed. She said she was looking forward to talking to me. What went wrong?

*What if's* started running rampant through my mind as I ate dinner in my room. I didn't dare think that she had changed her mind and didn't want to see me.

To distract my mind from the worrisome thoughts running and rerunning through my head, I finally turned on the TV and looked for a movie to watch until I fell asleep.

# Chapter 33

Morning dawned bright and clear. A cold front had moved in overnight and the temperature had dropped considerably since yesterday. I made a quick stop at Wal-Mart for heavier winter clothes, including gloves and a hat. After a hot breakfast at a sit-down restaurant, I went back to my room. About 9:00 a.m., my phone rang. There were only three people I expected to get calls from and I preferred them in this order: Christy, Phillip, and Hilary. Naturally, the call was from the last person on the list I wanted to talk to.

"Hello, Hilary."

"Gregory, we need to talk," she demanded. "Come to the house right away. I'll be in the kitchen."

"Wait!" I shouted before she could hang up.

"What is it?" she asked impatiently.

"I'd rather not come to the house. Let's meet somewhere else."

She sighed. I could see her rolling her eyes in frustration. "Why don't you want to come to the house? It's your house, too, you know."

"I know, I know. It's just . . . I feel uncomfortable there. I feel like a stranger in someone else's house because I still don't have Greg's memories. If you want to meet, it will have to be somewhere else."

She let out a loud sigh. "Fine," she snapped. "Do you

have someplace in mind?"

I wanted to shout, *How could I? You just called.* Instead, I calmly said, "No, but I'll call you back in three minutes and tell you where to meet me." I quickly hung up before she could argue.

I Googled restaurants near me, then chose one about two miles away. I didn't want one too close to my motel. For some unknown reason that I couldn't explain, I didn't want her to know where I was staying. I called her back, gave her the name and address of the restaurant, and told her to meet me there in an hour-and-a-half. I needed time to mentally prepare myself for the meeting . . . by taking a little nap.

* * *

I made sure I got to the restaurant first. I wanted to be seated in an out-of-the-way booth so we'd have plenty of privacy. I'd timed it so we would be there between the morning breakfast crowd and the lunch crowd. I was happy to see that there were plenty of tables and booths available. I was drinking coffee when Hilary entered the building.

She saw me, but instead of coming straight to my table, she stopped and said something to a waitress. The waitress nodded and headed toward the kitchen.

As Hilary got closer to the table, I noticed she carried a manila folder in one hand. *Oh, oh, that can't be good news.*

Hilary had a bounce in her step and looked like she was in a good mood. Her haughty, high-and-mighty attitude flowed around her like a billowing gown. "Good morning, Gregory," she said as she slid onto the red vinyl bench seat opposite me. She set her purse on the seat. She placed the folder on the table, squarely in front of her.

"Hello," I replied, wondering what was coming next.

"How have you been?" she asked, slipping her coat off her shoulders and laying it over her purse on the bench seat.

"Fine." The tab on the folder had one word on it: Lake Havasu. *Lake Havasu? I have a really bad feeling about this.*

"Hmmm, not very talkative today, are we?"

"Not really," I replied warily.

About that time, the waitress came to the table. She had an ice tea in one hand and a coffee pot in the other. Now, I knew what Hilary had arranged with her. She set Hilary's tea on a napkin on the table next to the folder. Hilary gave the waitress a dirty look and moved the folder over so the condensation from the glass wouldn't get the folder wet. "Other than some privacy, that will be all for now," Hilary told the waitress as if she was dismissing some of her hired help.

The waitress gave me a wow-she's-full-of-herself-look as she filled my coffee cup. She quickly turned and left.

"I have a message from your father," Hilary said, pouring a package of artificial sweetener into her ice tea. "He says to quit . . . and I'm quoting here . . . 'quit screwing around and get your ass back to work.' "

"Oh, that's a loving message if I ever heard one. Tell the old fart to jump off a bridge, preferably with gold bricks attached to his feet."

Her eyes narrowed in anger. "He is your father, Gregory. He only wants what's best for you." She placed one hand on the folder, as if it had precious information in it and she was afraid it would get stolen off the table.

"No, he wants what's best for his financial bottom line. He wants me to get my memories back so I can go back to work, and he can go back to being retired while

I'm making all the money."

"Speaking of family," she said, changing the subject. "William wants to see you." Her fingers drummed lightly on the folder.

I thought hard for a moment. "And, if I remember right, William is . . . one of our kids?" I asked hesitantly.

She sighed. "Yes, our middle child. He's been trying to take your place in the company office, but he's not ready to take over yet. That's why your father has been helping out. Your father and William ask me every day if you have your memories back. They both think that, if you go back to work, it will help your memory." She paused. When I didn't say anything, she added, "They could be right, you know? William wants to talk to you about the Standall Enterprises deal. Apparently, there are some last-minute concerns and he's not sure how to handle them. Maybe if you get involved, it would help jumpstart your memories." Toying with me, she lifted one corner of the folder, almost high enough for me to get a little glimpse inside, but not quite.

I held my hand up, staving off her protest about having me meet with William. "I'm not sure that's a good idea. I know he's Greg's son . . . my son . . . and all, but I still think of myself as Brad. I don't have Greg's memories, which means I don't remember William. Meeting with him would be like meeting a complete stranger, not my son. Besides, I wouldn't know the first thing about the kind of business deal he's working on. He'd be better off asking dear old daddy for help."

As though she had expected that kind of response from me, she shrugged. "Whatever. If that's how you feel, fine. I will tell William." She slid the folder back and forth on the table, an inch each way, as if she was purposely trying to draw my attention to it.

"Okay, Hilary, I'll bite. What's in the folder?"

She gave me a fake, surprised look. "What? This

folder? Are you anxious to see what's in here?" She picked it up and waved it back and forth.

"About as anxious as a condemned man standing on the gallows waiting for the bottom to drop out from underneath him," I said. "I have a feeling whatever's in it is not good news for me. You might as well show me and get it over with."

"Before I show you what's in here, remind me again, did you meet anyone you knew in your alternate life while you were in Lake Havasu?" She took a sip of her tea, staring intently at me over the rim of the glass.

*Oh, oh, does she know about Christy? How could she?* I didn't dare say yes or no. "Enough with the games, Hilary. If you have something to show me, just show it to me."

"See for yourself," she said, pushing the folder toward me.

My heart raced as I reached for it. Picking up the folder, I opened it. Everything around me slowed down. Sounds diminished until the only thing I could hear was the rushing of blood in my ears. My vision narrowed, zooming in on the only thing in the folder. A single picture. And what a picture it was. It showed me, standing next to the stage under the London Bridge, kissing Christy. There was no denying it was me. Whoever took the picture was good, a fully recognizable shot of me.

"What the hell?" I said as soon as I regained my composure. I put the folder on the table in front of me.

"I'd say this is an interesting development in your trip to Lake Havasu, isn't it?"

"How . . . when . . . did . . . ?" That bearded guy in the Elks and the Eagles who kept watching me. I knew something wasn't right with him. Once I got my mouth working, I blurted, "What did you do? Hire a private investigator?"

She shrugged and said proudly, "Of course. Would you expect anything less of me?"

"I guess I should have at least suspected you'd pull something like this. But you know what? It doesn't matter. What's done is done. So where do we go from here?" I sat back and folded my arms across my chest. I was furious and feared I might pick up something and throw it at her.

"It's really very simple, Gregory," she said in a condescending voice. "You forget about your life as Brad, including your little girlfriend. You come back to the house. We go back to what we had before you had your accident. If you agree to that, this folder and the rest of the pictures and negatives I have, magically disappear."

"And if I don't agree?"

"Timothy files a divorce on infidelity grounds," she hissed. "And I promise you, Gregory, I will fight tooth-and-nail to see you destroyed. I will do whatever it takes to see you broke, financially as well as mentally."

*Wow. What a cold-hearted woman. What am I supposed to say to that?* It had become more and more apparent to me that she cared more about the money and her position in society than she ever cared about Greg or their marriage.

Obviously, I wasn't going to agree to her terms. There was no way I could live with her. Whatever her arrangement with Greg before his accident, nothing was going to be the same in either of our lives with me around. I was now Brad.

Since she had mentioned she would make sure I was financially ruined, I considered that I had earned all that money she enjoyed spending. Even if I didn't remember making the money, I felt I deserved something out of it, at least enough to tide me over while I was getting settled in Havasu. I felt sure Phillip could get me enough to cover what I would need for a while.

Silent for once, Hilary sat with a smug look on her face.

I glanced around and caught the waitress's attention. When she got to the table, I pulled out my wallet and said, "I need to leave. It's an emergency. Will this cover the bill?" I put a twenty on the table.

"Yes, and then some," the waitress said with a smile.

"Good. Keep the change." I slid out of my seat, taking the folder with me.

"What do you think you're doing, Gregory?" Hilary demanded, sitting up straight and eyeing the folder.

"Oh, mind if I borrow this?" I held the folder up. "I think my attorney would like to see it. I'll be in touch." I turned and walked away before she could reply. No sense in sitting here, arguing about the whole thing.

She'd shown her hand. Now it was time for me and Phillip to come up with a counter attack. But before I talked to him, I wanted to talk to Christy and make sure she was okay. If Hilary was crazy enough to have me followed, would she stoop to other lows, too?

# Chapter 34

I was really beginning to worry about Christy. I needed to know if she was just screening my calls or if something had happened to her. If she was screening my calls, I wanted to know why. What had happened between the time when I had arrived at the airport here and later that night, when she didn't answer her phone?

Now that Hilary knew about Christy, I was even more worried about her. I didn't know how far Hilary would go to protect her precious image. I didn't think she'd go so far as to have Christy hurt, but I didn't know for sure.

I bought a pre-paid phone card and went back to my room. Using the card, a number that Christy wouldn't recognize, I called her cell number.

"Hello?" she answered in a drowsy, half-awake voice.

"Christy! Don't hang up, please! I need to talk to you. Are you okay?"

"Brad?"

"Yeah."

She was silent so long, if it hadn't been for the faint background noise, I would have thought she'd hung up. Being a work day, I had assumed she would be at work, but her voice sounded like she'd just woken up.

"Are you okay?" I asked.

Another pause. Finally, she said, "I'm not sure I

should be talking to you."

"No, no, no," I said. "At least tell me why. Are you okay? You're not hurt or anything are you? Is it something I said or did? I thought we were heading toward something special. Then suddenly, you wouldn't answer your phone. I think I deserve an explanation." I didn't know if it was that part about heading toward something special or not, but I was encouraged that she didn't hang up.

"I'm fine, now," she said in a slightly stronger voice.

"What do you mean? What are you talking about?"

"Tuesday, after we talked . . . something happened."

She was so hesitant to talk, I feared she'd met another man or something. "Go on," I said.

"As I was getting in my car from work, two men approached me." Her voice lowered to a whisper so quiet I could barely hear her. "They threatened me, Brad. They said if I ever talked to you again, bad things would happen to me and my family. They were scary, Brad. Really, really scary."

*Hilary. It had to be Hilary.* "Damn it, Hilary," I hissed between clenched teeth.

"What?"

"Hilary. It had to be her doing. She had me followed. Today, she showed me a picture of us standing under the bridge kissing. Needless to say, I was totally shocked."

"She must have suspected from the beginning you might find me. Maybe she wanted to be prepared to gather evidence against you." Her voice was weak. Like she had no energy.

I hated to think that because of me she was going through such a hard time. "I'll talk to my attorney. Maybe we can get a restraining order or something to keep her and her thugs away from you."

"It's not just me, Brad. Those two guys know where my sister and her family live. They know where my mom lives. They know who my friends are. That's why I can't take the chance of seeing you again. I wouldn't be able to live with myself if something happened to someone I know because of something I did."

I heard beeping noises in the background. "Where are you?"

She hesitated, then reluctantly said, "I'm in the hospital."

"*What?*" I exclaimed in shock. "Are you okay? What happened?"

"One of those guys that approached me had a gun."

"Did he shoot you?" I stammered in disbelief. *Oh, my god. I can't believe she's been shot.* I sat down on the bed. My hands shook. I could hardly hold the phone to my ear.

"I don't think he meant to. He was waving the gun around, threatening me and my family, and it went off. I think it shocked him as much as it did me." She tried to laugh a little, but it was forced.

"But you're okay, right?"

"The bullet hit me in the shoulder. It didn't hit anything vital. I've been on pain meds and, until yesterday, I wasn't in any shape to talk to anyone. I told Trina to bring me my cell phone, but she wouldn't."

That explained why Christy hadn't answered her phone for the last three days.

"By the way, Trina's dead set against me having anything to do with you. She took my purse and phone to my house so they wouldn't be laying around here. She wouldn't bring my phone back because she knew I'd call you. I finally talked my sister into going to my apartment and bringing it to me this morning."

Sister? The Crissy I remembered from Greg's made-up life didn't have a sister. In fact, I don't remember her having any family. "You have family in Havasu?"

"Yeah. My mom is Trina—"

"Trina's your mom?" I started laughing.

"I know. She can be annoying at times, but she means well."

"Well, she certainly cares a lot about you." Half-jokingly, I added, "I'm surprised she's not knocking on my door to kick my butt."

"If she thought you had anything to do with me getting shot, she would be at your door. As it is, I've had to threaten her to keep her from searching out who did this to me. I told her to leave it up to the police. They'll figure out who told those guys to threaten me and take care of it."

"I'm sure they will," I said, my mind reeling at the implications. "What about the rest of your family? I didn't know you had family."

"My dad and my step-mom are here. My sister, her husband and their kids live here, too. My brother lives in San Diego with his wife and kids."

"I'll be looking forward to meeting them all," I said as I realized that being with Christy would take me way beyond Brad's imagined world.

Despite Hilary's cold, mean streak, I couldn't picture her doing something this drastic, but apparently she had. I wasn't going to let her get away with it. "Give me a chance to fix this, okay? I'm going to talk to my attorney." I looked at my watch. "This late, I may not be able to get an appointment until tomorrow morning."

She didn't say anything right away. "You won't tell anyone other than your attorney that we talked, will you?"

"No. This phone call is between you and me. I'll take all necessary precautions to keep it that way. Are we good?"

"Yes," she said. "Go ahead and talk to him. But I don't think there's anything he will be able to do."

"If he can't, I'll find someone who *can* do

something," I said. "I'm not letting you go without a fight. And I'll fight to the death for you, Christy. I'll call you when I hear something, okay?"

In a shaky voice, she said, "Okay." It sounded almost like she was crying.

As soon as we said our good-byes, I hung up the phone and called Phillip's office. His answering machine picked up. At the beep, I said, "Phillip, it's Brad. A major development just reared its ugly head. I need to see you as soon as possible. Call me." I left my number and hung up.

I wondered how Hilary could have stooped so low. I never would have imagined she would be capable of hiring thugs to threaten Christy. And where would she find them, anyway?

It dawned on me that she'd told me that Nick and Stella still had contacts with their old gang. That was a possible resource for her. Another thought passed through my mind. Maybe dear old dad had something to do with this. He would have had a lot of contacts over the years, and I wouldn't have put it past him to get involved in shady deals. He might have worried with Hilary that a divorce would hurt the business and radically affect his retirement income. They were the main two people who would have a big stake in my interest in Christy.

But somehow, Hilary stood out as the one most likely to instigate the plan because of her desire for money and social status. And I was a threat to both.

# Chapter 35

The next morning, Phillip took me straight into his office. After we got seated, he said, "So, what's up?"

"You won't believe what Hilary's done."

"That bad?"

I told him what had happened to Christy.

"Oookaaay," he said. "Looks like they're going to get down and dirty right away."

I told him about Nick and Stella, and how they were former gang members. "I would guess Hilary went through them to have this done. The question is, can we do anything to prevent it from happening again?"

"Yeah, there's probably something we can do. Let me contact the police in Havasu to get the whole story."

"I'm really worried Hilary will have Christy or some of her family hurt. She threatened me yesterday about going ahead with the divorce. She could use Christy or her family to retaliate."

"Give me a few hours this morning to talk to the police and see what I can come up with."

"Great. Oh, I just thought about something . . . . Do you think Hilary would go so far as to put a hold on the bank accounts?"

He mulled it over for a few seconds. "Very possible. It would be a good way to force you back to her. It would take away the only means you have to survive on your own at this point."

"Can you do something about that, too?"

"No, but you can," he said with a smirk.

"Me? What can I do?"

He leaned forward on the desk. "Go to your bank, any branch. It doesn't have to be the branch you and Hilary use now. Open an account in your name only. Then, transfer some money over to the new account. She can't touch it if she's not on the account."

"Can I do that?"

"Sure you can. It's your money. If she can use it, you can use it. You can do whatever you want with it."

Technically it was my money, if I thought of myself as Greg. And yesterday, that thought had occurred to me when Hilary said she would ruin me financially. But now, I was feeling like Brad. It seemed like I would be stealing someone else's money if I did what Phillip was suggesting. "I guess I could do it," I said, but not very convincingly.

"You have ID proving you're Greg, don't you?"

"Sure. Hilary gave me Greg's wallet. I have a driver's license, credit cards, and I don't know what else. I haven't looked that closely."

"So do it," he said. "Protect yourself while you can."

I pondered the idea for a moment. "How much do you think I should move? Ten thousand?"

He laughed. "Get real, Brad. You're a multi-millionaire. I'd say at least a million, five would be better."

"Five?" I asked in surprise. "That's a lot of money. I wouldn't be comfortable taking that much from her. I'd feel like I was stealing it from her."

"See, you're not thinking like Greg. You're thinking like Brad. But for now, you are Greg. Use it to your advantage and take the money before she cuts you off.

Do it soon. You can always give part of the five million back later if you don't need it."

He was right about that. I didn't have to keep the money if I wasn't comfortable having that much. And I needed to do this now, before Hilary thought to lock me out of the accounts. "Okay. I'll go as soon as I leave here. But I'm only going to do two million." I got up to leave.

"What address are you going to give the bank?" Phillip asked casually.

"Address?"

"Yeah. You can't very well have them send the paperwork and a debit card to Hilary's house."

I felt like an idiot. That would have been a stupid move, especially if I was sitting at the bank and I didn't have an address to give them.. "You're right. They'll need to send me a debit card so I'll be able to access the account at ATM's."

Phillip picked up a pen and wrote something on a piece of paper. Standing up, he handed it to me across the desk. "Use the address of my office here. If anything comes in, I'll get it to you."

"Thanks." Relief flooded through me. I was glad I'd found such a smart lawyer.

He handed me the pen and pad of paper. "Before you go, give me Christy's phone number. I need to talk to her about what happened the other day and see who she's talked to at the police department."

I wrote her number down, gave it to him, and headed out the door.

Since I didn't know which bank or branch Hilary and Greg used, I dug Greg's wallet out of my pocket. All the credit cards had Chase stamped on them. His debit card also came from Chase. That meant he had at least a checking account there. It didn't guarantee that that account held two million dollars, but it seemed like the best possibility. I drove to the closest branch, hoping Greg hadn't visited there regularly and that I wouldn't be recognized.

\* \* \*

I walked into the front door of the bank and noticed right away that it wasn't busy. One customer stood at the counter and one sat at a desk. The good news was, there were plenty of employees available to help me. The bad news was, I couldn't blend into a crowd.

A young woman approached me. Her high heels clicked on the tile floor. "Hello, welcome to Chase Bank. How may I help you today?" She looked to be in her twenties with long dark hair and brown eyes. She wore a black, knee-length skirt and a white blouse. Plain, but functional attire for a business woman.

"I have several accounts with you," I said off the top of my head, not knowing if that was really true. But once the words had escaped my mouth, it was too late to worry about it. I would soon find out. All I could do was move forward and hope for the best. "I need to open another account and transfer some money from an existing account into it."

"No problem," she said, motioning me toward an empty desk and couple of chairs. "I can help you with that." She sat at the desk, fiddled with the mouse for a moment, clicked some buttons and tapped a few keys. "Okay," she said, "let's get started."

I gave her my ID and the debit card for good measure. So far, no one seemed to recognize me and everything was going okay, but I was still nervous.

As a list of accounts came up on the computer screen, the young woman's eyes widened in surprise. "It looks like you have multiple accounts with us. All of them with substantial amounts of money in them."

"Yes," I replied as casually as I could, sweat running down my back. "I want to open a new account . . . in my name only, and transfer two million dollars into it. I don't care which account you take the money from."

"That shouldn't be a problem," she said, tapping at her keyboard. "Give me just a minute to open a new account and put this information into the computer."

I tried not to fidget while she worked, but it was hard to sit there, not knowing if this was going to fly or not. If I could have paced the room while she typed, it would have helped relieve my growing stress.

Finally, she said, "Okay, I need to go get the paperwork from the printer. I'll be right back."

She returned shortly with a small stack of papers in her hand. Sitting down, she sorted through them, setting some in front of her and setting others to the side. "Okay, I need your signature on these three papers and we'll be done." She slid the first paper across the desk. She pointed to where I was supposed to sign, then handed me the pen.

I broke out in a cold sweat, trying to hide my nervousness. I fought to keep my hand from shaking too much and dropping the pen in front of the woman. I hadn't thought about having to sign Greg's name. I knew how to sign Brad's name, I could picture doing it in my mind. I had no idea how Greg signed his name. Did he sign it Greg or Gregory? Did he use a middle initial? This could be bad, very bad. If I screwed this up, no doubt she would call the cops and I would end up in jail. I didn't know what to do.

"Is something wrong?" she asked, concern showing in her eyes.

"No, I . . . was just reading it before I sign. Can't be too careful these days," I said, hoping I sounded convincing.

"Rrright," she muttered, her mouth and eyes tightening up in what looked like a suspicious leer.

I had to sign. So, without thinking about it, I signed Gregory Nordmeyer, letting my subconscious mind guide my hand.

"Great," she said, taking the paper and sliding another one into its place in front of me. Only two more to go and you're done."

Once again, I let my subconscious take over for the remaining signatures. When I was done, I sat back while she looked the forms over. Her brow wrinkled in concentration, confusion, then doubt, which flashed across her face as her eyes flicked from the paperwork to me. I about had a heart attack when she picked up my ID and said, "I need to verify your signature. I'll be right back."

"Is there something wrong with it?"

She paused, saying nothing, confirming my suspicion that she thought there was something wrong.

Laughing, I added, "I signed the right name, didn't I?"

She looked at the paperwork. "Yes, you did. But company policy requires me to check the signatures when this much money is involved in a transaction. It's nothing to worry about."

Taking the paperwork and my ID with her, she got up and left. She walked behind the tellers' counter, opened a door, and disappeared inside a room. I was convinced that, as soon as she got inside, she would pick up a phone and call the cops.

From where I was sitting, I couldn't see the entrance doors because they were around a corner. But I listened closely for every time the doors opened. And every time they opened, I thought, O*kay, this is it.* I expected four cops to come storming through the door with guns drawn. They would grab me, throw me to the ground, handcuff me, and haul me off to jail.

After what seemed like hours, the woman came out the door. An older man in a suit and tie followed her. They stopped and she pointed at me. The man held my ID in his hand. He stared hard, his eyes moving from me to my ID.

Impulsively, I slid forward on my seat, ready to bolt for the door. I figured I could be out the door, in my car, and gone before they could catch up to me. Just as I tensed my legs to stand up, he smiled, nodded his head to the woman, and handed her my ID.

Smiling, she came toward me.

I slid back in my chair, concentrating on slowing my racing heart and shaking body. Sweat ran down my forehead. My armpits felt like a rain forest.

"Okay, you're all set, Mr. Nordmeyer," she said, handing me a folder with my paperwork in it. "Don't forget your ID and debit card." She held them out to me. "Is there anything else we can do for you today?"

I wanted to say, *No, you've already given me enough stress for one day.* "No, I think this will do it."

"Then you have a nice day," she said, walking me to the door.

"You, too," I replied, replacing my ID and debit card in my wallet.

I sat in the car for a full five minutes, waiting for my body to quit shaking so I could drive.

# Chapter 36

Two weeks later, Phillip and I sat in an unused conference room at the courthouse, where we were having our first meeting with Hilary and her attorney, Timmy.

"Gregory," Hilary said as she came into the room, followed closely by Timmy. "Are you ready for this?"

"No problem." I tried to sound cool and calm as I responded, but inside I was nervous about how Hilary was going to react today to the things on the agenda Phillip and I had prepared. "It's going to be a piece of cake."

She cocked her head and looked at me sideways. "Pretty confident, are you?"

I smiled at her. "How's it going, Timmy?"

He glared at me and slammed his briefcase down on the table.

Hilary was dressed to the hilt. Her linen skirt and silk blouse were white. Her high-heeled shoes and expensive purse were white. She looked like the ice queen. Her manner matched her looks, cold and cruel. There was also a haughtiness about her that said, *I hold all the cards.*

Timmy wore a dark-blue three-piece suit with a red tie. *Symbolizing what?* I thought. *Tearing out of the throat?*

Phillip and I had dressed casually in jeans and short-sleeved button-up shirts. No ties or jackets.

Hilary looked at Phillip's clothes and smirked, like he was a joke.

Once everyone was seated, Timmy started laying out their demands. "First, Hilary and the rest of the family are insisting that Gregory see a psychiatrist until such time as he regains the memories of his past. Second, we are going to get a restraining order on everyone Gregory came into contact with in Lake Havasu. We believe they are trying to scam him out of a large portion of money. Third, he will not be allowed to work until such time as he can prove he is capable of—"

A sudden, loud knock sounded at the door.

"This room is being used," Timmy shouted.

Phillip stood up. "I think this is for us." He walked over and opened the door.

A tall, well-built man with short dark hair stepped into the room. He wore tan slacks, a tan sports jacket over a blue button-up shirt, and a yellow tie. He held a manila folder in his hand.

Hilary's eyes darted from the folder to me and back to the folder. Just like me at the restaurant, she was worried about what it contained.

"This meeting is supposed to be between you and me and our clients," Timmy whined to Phillip.

"I realize that," Phillip said, "but this man has information that will change your outlook on the proceedings."

"This is highly irregular. I must tell you—"

"Just give me five minutes," Phillip said. "After that, if you think he should leave, he will."

Timmy looked at Hilary for approval.

"Fine," she snarled, "But I'm warning you, if he is not out of here in five minutes, I'll throw him out myself."

The tall man smiled at her.

Phillip said, "First, let me introduce him. Hilary, Timothy, this is Lieutenant Burns."

Hilary's mouth dropped open and her eyes got big. It was priceless. Sitting up straight, she stuttered, as if she was trying to find a nice way to say something like, *I didn't really mean it when I said I'd throw you out of the room. Please don't arrest me for being insolent.* She finally got herself under control and sat back in her chair.

Timmy on the other hand just had to butt in. "What's the meaning of this? Why is this man here?"

Lieutenant Burns took over. "I'm from the Lake Havasu City Arizona Police Department. I'm here to question your client about a crime that happened in Lake Havasu. I have a room reserved across the hall." He gestured to Hilary. "Would you come with me, please?"

Hilary stared at him for a moment, maybe trying to make the connection between her and Havasu. She looked at Timmy for advice.

Timmy said, "He's an officer of the law. There's nothing I can do. I'll go with you."

"No," she barked, stopping Timmy before he could get out of his chair. "I'll take care of this." Moaning and grumbling under her breath about the inconvenience of the whole thing, Hilary followed the lieutenant out the door.

I wondered if she wanted to keep Timmy out of her business with Lake Havasu. In her mind, she probably thought she hadn't done anything wrong. At least, nothing that could be traced to her.

As soon as they left, two more men entered the room. One of them held a folder that was a twin to the one Lieutenant Burns had carried.

The first man said, "I'm Detective Roth of the Lake Havasu City Police Department." He nodded at the other man. "This is Officer Jamison of the White Plains Police

Department. While my partner is talking to Ms. Nordmeyer, I will explain why we're here."

Phillip and I knew why they were there. Timmy, on the other hand, was about to get blindsided. I couldn't wait to see what was going to happen.

Arrogantly, Timmy leaned back in his chair and folded his arms across his chest.

Detective Roth said to him, "Your client, Ms. Nordmeyer, did something she shouldn't have done." He opened the folder and started reading. "At five-ten p.m., on Wednesday, October 8, as Christy Thayer was leaving work, two males approached her."

"Who is Christy Thayer?" Timmy interrupted, looking from me and Phillip to Detective Roth.

"Let's not play games," Detective Roth growled. "I'm sure your client has shown you the photo of Brad kissing Christy under the London Bridge. Hasn't she?" He glared at Timmy, who backed down quickly, shocked at being treated so rudely.

The detective continued. "Hilary gave her hired handyman, Nick, five grand, and asked him to find someone to . . . and I'm quoting here . . . 'make sure Christy never contacts Gregory again.' Nick immediately contacted a member of his old gang in Chicago, who in turn, contacted someone he knows in Vegas, who in turn, contacted two young men in Lake Havasu. These two young men used a gun to force Christy against her car where they proceeded to threatened to kill her and certain members of her family if she saw or talked to Brad again."

Timmy stared at Detective Roth in shock. He remained silent.

"Unfortunately for Hilary, while waving the gun around, it went off and one of the men accidentally shot Christy."

Timmy's eyes widened and his face got pale.

"Fortunately for us, these two men were not the sharpest knives in the drawer. Before she got shot, Christy overheard them say their names. With her description of them and their first names, it wasn't hard to find them. After a short," he chuckled, "a very short interrogation of them, they spilled everything. They told us who hired them. It didn't take long to trace the path back to Hilary."

Timmy sat up. "Do you have proof of this?" he demanded.

Detective Roth threw the folder on the table. "It's all there. If you need a minute to look it over, take it."

We all waited in silence as Timmy scanned through the documents. The further he read, the redder his face grew. When he was done, he said, "I need to talk to my client. In private."

"No problem," Phillip said, amused. "When Lieutenant Burns is done questioning Hilary, you can use the same conference room they are using now. It's right across the hall. Take your time. We'll be here." He smiled.

The door opened. Ashen-faced Hilary entered, followed by Lieutenant Burns. There was still a haughtiness in her manner, even though she looked a little shaken.

Detective Roth said, "That didn't take long. We good?"

Lieutenant Burns nodded. "Yes, we are." He looked at Timmy. "You may want to have a talk with your client."

Timmy stood up, gathering the folder and its contents. "Hilary," he said sharply, "come with me."

Without a word, she followed him out the door.

Lieutenant Burns and Phillip gave me big smiles and two thumbs up.

\* \* \*

Hilary entered the room ahead of Timothy. She'd been surprised by what Lieutenant Burns had said about Christy getting shot. She hadn't been too worried about it. She'd only hired the people to scare Christy, not shoot her or kill her. If the thugs took it further than she had intended, that was their problem, not hers. She was confident Timothy could fix it so she would be in the clear.

Timothy waved the folder in the air as soon as the door closed behind him. "What about this, Hilary? Tell me it isn't true."

"I assure you, Timothy, they have nothing," she said, taking a seat at the table.

He walked to the table and stood next to her chair. "Did you hire someone to threaten this woman?" His pinched face showed that he already knew the answer.

"Of course. I wasn't about to sit back and let some floozy take my husband away from me without a fight, especially when he's confused about who he is. You know me better than that."

"Is that what you told the officer?"

"Well, he was asking me all kinds of questions about my relationship with our maintenance man, Nick, and if I paid him to have someone scare off that low-life woman who was trying to take my husband. I didn't see a reason not to be truthful."

He threw the folder on the table. "Do you know what's in there, Hilary?"

"Does it matter?" she asked, looking at the folder. She hadn't paid that much attention to Lieutenant Burns because she didn't see how they had anything serious on her.

He pulled out the chair next to her and sat down. Tapping the folder with the index finger of his right hand, he said, "If everything in this folder checks out, there is enough evidence to send you to prison for at least two years. They have an arrest warrant and extradition papers."

"Prison? Just for having someone put a scare into a gold-digging slut who is trying to steal my husband? Don't make me laugh."

"Hilary, I don't think you understand. That lieutenant is going to arrest you. Today. And take you back to Lake Havasu."

A sudden chill ran through her. She sat up straight and looked at him. "That can't be right. All I did was have somebody warn her away from him. It can't be that serious of a charge. Surely nothing more than a slap on the wrist."

"Hilary, they didn't just *talk* to her. They used a gun to threaten her with serious bodily harm and death. And they shot her."

"I didn't tell them to do that. Besides, it wasn't intentional."

"It's called conspiracy to commit murder. It's a class-one felony and carries a sentence of five to fifteen years in prison. Did you think it wouldn't come out during the divorce proceedings? How could you be so stupid, Hilary?"

"Well, can't you fix it? You are the best lawyer in town. You can fix these things."

In a frustrated tone, he said, "A lot depends on how willing they are to work with us. Although the words 'make sure Christy never contacts Gregory again,' didn't mention murder, they imply it. I know you didn't actually hire them to murder her, so I might be able to get it down to less than five years. Would you be willing to plead guilty and take a year or two of probation?"

She jumped to her feet, knocking her chair over backwards. "Absolutely not! That would ruin me socially. Not to mention what effect it might have on the company."

"It might be the easiest way to make this go away."

"No. There has to be something else you can do."

He picked up the folder. "Let me look at these papers again." He opened the folder and started reading.

Thankful for a few quiet minutes to regroup her turbulent mind, Hilary righted her chair with shaky hands and sat down.

*Prison?* she thought. *I can't go to prison. What would my family think? What would my friends think? Even probation would ruin me socially. Timothy has to fix this.* If he couldn't, she would find another way. Between her, her parents, and Gregory's parents, they had enough contacts that she could be sure she would be able to smooth everything over and get out of this mess with nothing more than a slight tarnishing of her reputation. It was just a desperate woman's mistake. People would understand.

After what seemed like a long wait, Timothy closed the folder. "This is bad, Hilary. They have signed confessions from everybody involved. From your handyman to his cousin in Chicago, to his brother in Las Vegas, to the two guys who actually threatened her. Once the two in Havasu caved in and told who had hired them, everybody else passed the buck along. Everybody was willing to give up the person above them in order to diminish their own involvement."

"So, what does all that mean to me?" Hilary demanded.

"It means you are going to be arrested and taken to Lake Havasu today."

Hilary's face drained of color. She started shaking. "Arrested? Me? That's not right. I'm rich. Rich people don't get arrested. Do something, Timothy."

"If you don't plea bargain, there's not a lot I can do. They have the arrest warrant and the extradition papers in order. I could try to take it to a judge and have the papers rescinded, but that's a long-shot."

After a pause, he went on. "I'm sure Gregory and Phillip are going to have certain terms they will want you to agree to for the divorce. Maybe if you agree to their terms, they will be able to lower some of the charges."

Hilary pursed her lips. "In other words, it's go to jail or give in to whatever they want."

He nodded as he sat back. "I'm afraid so. I might be good, but I can only do so much within the law."

A scary thought suddenly occurred to her. "What if he wants all the money, the house, everything? Can he do that?"

"He can't take everything. You have certain rights, too. But he could demand at least half of everything, including the house."

"Can you negotiate with them if they ask for too much?"

"I'm sure I can. Although I don't know how firm they are going to be. We'll just have to wait and see what they put on the table. Unfortunately, you may not have a lot of bargaining room with this case hanging over you."

She sat in silence a moment, trying to gather herself. Her hands shook. She said hesitantly, "I guess we'd better go see what they want." She stood up and moved toward the door. "Let's get this over with."

"Oh, and one more thing, Hilary," Timothy said tightly, picking the folder up from the table. "Before we go back in there, is there anything else you've done that I should know about?" He looked her in the eye.

"No," she immediately responded, feeling humiliated by the accusation in his voice. "Nothing."

"Good. Because, as your attorney, I'm warning you, if you lie to me, or withhold information from me again at any time, I will let them take you to prison, friends or not. Understand?" His tone of voice said that he meant every word.

She felt the blood drain from her face at the thought of going to prison, even for a day or two, let alone two years.

As they walked out of the room, she thought, *In retrospect, I probably shouldn't have tried to scare off that woman. Things might have worked out the way I wanted in the end anyway. At least, I would have gotten the house and all the money. But what is done is done.*

All she could do now was find out what Gregory wanted. If he was bound and determined to divorce her, fine. She'd let him go. But she wasn't about to let it ruin her socially or financially.

True, the divorce might tarnish her reputation a little. Lots of people she knew had gotten divorces. But her parents had instilled in her the fact that a marriage was forever and if she got a divorce, it meant she had failed. Failure was not an option in her parents' eyes. Society would be more lenient on her. But in her heart, she would always know that she had failed.

*     *     *

When Hilary came back in the room, her face was as white as her silk blouse. She looked scared. I hoped she was as scared as Christy had been when she was held at gunpoint and shot.

The two officers from Lake Havasu had remained in the room and were seated, awaiting the completion of the meeting.

As Hilary and Timmy took their seats, Timmy said, "So, I take it you have certain terms you want to lay out for us?"

"Yes, we do," Phillip said, standing up and opening his briefcase. He pulled out a sheet of paper. "First, Brad wants a total of ten million dollars, which would include the two million he transferred into his personal account two weeks ago."

Hilary's head whipped around to me. Apparently, she hadn't discovered the money transfer.

"Hold up a moment," Timmy said. "Why are you referring to him as Brad?"

Phillip smiled and pulled another paper out of his briefcase. Laying it on the table, he said, "Second, Gregory Nordmeyer no longer exists. This is a signed court order, officially changing his name to Brad Jones. A certified copy will be filed with the divorce papers. I'm going to have to insist that you use his correct name from now on."

Hilary blurted, "But what about—"

Phillip cut her off. "Third, once we leave this meeting, Brad wants no more contact whatsoever with any of Greg's family. This includes Hilary, their three children, Greg's parents, etcetera, etcetera." He pulled yet another paper from his briefcase. "Last, but not least, we have here a restraining order, forbidding Hilary or anyone within the family to contact, harass, or in any way communicate with Christy Thayer, her family, or friends." He closed the brief case and sat back in his chair.

"That's it? That's all you want?" Timmy asked in shock.

"Yes," I said. "That's all I want."

Timmy looked at Hilary, who seemed to be in shock, too. He turned to Lieutenant Burns. "And if we accept these terms, what happens to the charges contained in this folder?"

"If you accept the terms," Lieutenant Burns said, looking directly at Hilary, "I have a little wiggle room, but not a lot. Best case scenario: she pleads guilty to intimidation with a weapon and she gets a few years' probation. Either way, Detective Roth and I are going to have company on our flight back to Havasu."

Hilary looked at Timmy with desperation in her eyes. "Can't you do something? I can't be arrested. How will that look to everyone?" Her hands shook. She looked deathly white.

Ignoring her, Timmy said, "We accept your terms."

"*What*?" Hilary shot to her feet. "Don't let them do this." She turned to Lieutenant Burns." I want another attorney. I want to go in front of a judge here, in White Plains. In my own town—"

Her words trailed off as he pulled out his handcuffs.

"No," Hilary whispered, sinking down onto her chair.

Lieutenant Burns put the cuffs on her wrists and read her rights to her. At least, he was nice enough to put the cuffs in front of her.

I could only muster a little sympathy for her, knowing that she was going to have a rough road ahead. On the other hand, I felt justice was being done. A flood of relief flowed through my body. Once I left this room, I would be free of Hilary. I could go to Havasu to be with Christy.

"I guess we'll be leaving now," Lieutenant Burns said. He picked his folder up from the table. He turned toward the door with Hilary in tow. "Have a good day, everyone."

After the officers, with Hilary in tow, were gone, Phillip said to Timmy, "I'll send the paperwork to your office."

"That will be fine," Timmy replied stiffly. Stoically, he gathered up his paperwork and left.

I smiled to myself, remembering what Hilary had said about him, that he always resented Gregory's success, which came so easily, while Timmy had to work so hard. I'm sure this loss made more of an impact on him that he would have liked to admit.

"How long do you think it will take until the divorce goes through?" I asked Phillip.

"Since the terms have been agreed to, it should go pretty fast. For the general public, it takes about six weeks to go before a judge. But I know a few judges who handle divorce cases and I'll see if I can get it signed and sealed sooner. Either way, you'll be in Havasu, so I'll send you the papers you need to sign and it can all be done by fax or through the mail."

"Great," I said. "Now, could I have just a moment? I need to make a quick phone call."

"Take your time. I'll wait outside." Picking up the papers, he stuck them in his briefcase, closed it, and went out the door.

I dialed Christy's phone. When she answered, I said, "Everything went exactly as we'd planned."

"Great!" she replied enthusiastically. "So, when will you be coming to Havasu?"

"I'll leave the day after tomorrow. I need a day to wrap things up here."

"I can't wait to see you."

My heart soared. "I can't wait to see you, too. Love you."

"Love you, too."

# Chapter 37

Lake Havasu City, AZ
Three Years Later

Six children, ranging in ages from two to four, ran around the park and played, having the time of their lives. There was a bouncy house with a slide, a shallow pool full of toys, cake and ice cream, and for one lucky little two-year-old, birthday presents. The event? Our daughter Megan's birthday party.

Sitting at a picnic table in Rotary Park, I watched Christy and the other moms hover around the kids to look for any trouble that might pop up. It gave me time to reflect on the past three years.

After the meeting in New York, Hilary had pleaded guilty to the lesser charges and got off with two years' probation. I never did hear if it affected her socially, and I didn't care. As far as I was concerned, she got what she deserved.

The day after I had arrived in Havasu, I started making contacts in the construction world. I bought a house, a new pickup truck, all the tools I thought I would need for my work, and within a week, I was in business.

All in all, the last three years had been perfect. Well, with one little exception. After six months had passed, Greg's memories started invading my brain. Nothing major at first. Just little things, like seeing Disneyland on

TV, having a vague memory of being there with Hilary and the kids. As time moved on, the memories became more intense, more real.

Now, three years later, I had all of Greg's memories. It was like another life, but I didn't like it because I didn't want to be reminded of that life. I had put a lot of time and effort into creating this life before I left that one.

The intrusion of Greg's memories came often enough to keep Hilary and the kids in the back of my mind. I had been open to seeing the kids, so I had Phillip contact them. Jonathan and Brittney thought I was the worst kind of scum and never wanted to talk to me again. William wasn't as dead-set against me as the other two, and things might have worked out between us if Hilary and Greg's parents had left him alone. They convinced him to believe I would ruin his life if he had any contact with me. I let it go . . . for now. Maybe down the road, he and I could work things out.

Every now and then, when I would wonder how Hilary and the kids were doing, I would have to force them out of my mind. I wanted to focus on the people who were in my life now: Christy and Megan.

One good thing came from Greg's memories. I was a much better businessman now than I had been in my imaginary life as Brad. In that made-up alternate life, I didn't see myself as a great businessman. I got by, but nothing like now.

Greg's success spoke for itself. I used part of the money from the divorce to back a startup company belonging to a friend of mine. The company became a huge success. I invested the profits from that venture into another new startup I heard about from a friend. Once again, great success. True, I didn't have a hundred-million in the bank like Greg, but I had enough to live on for the rest of my life, and then some.

I set up a college fund for Megan that would cover all

expenses, no matter what college she went to in the future. She would also have access to a trust fund when she turned twenty-one.

I watched Trina getting ready to pass out cake and ice cream as Christy and the other moms herded the kids to a nearby picnic table. I was proud of Christy as a mother and proud of what she had become.

One night a couple of years ago, Christy had confided in me that she'd always wanted to be an author. Soon afterwards, she quit her job and started writing. She was now a bestselling-author with three books out and more on the way.

Our son, still three months away from making his big debut, will be able to do anything he wants in life. But I was hoping he'd want to work with me doing construction. Yup, even with all my success, I still enjoyed working with my hands. I will probably work until the day I die.

When the party was over and the mess cleaned up, we drove home. Megan, worn out from the day's activities, was asleep before I left the parking lot.

* * *

Later that evening, after dinner and after we put Megan to bed for the night, Christy and I did what we loved to do on a Sunday. We cuddled up on the couch in the dark and watched a movie.

Christy kept wriggling and moving her feet around.

Having enough of that, I paused the movie. "What's wrong? You're antsier than a bride on her wedding night."

"If you would stop touching my feet, I wouldn't move around so much."

"Sweetie, I'm not touching you."

"You're not?" She looked at me with big eyes.

"No, I'm trying to watch the movie."

"This is really strange," she said. "I keep having this really funny feeling on my feet."

Déjà vu washed over me. "Oh, oh. What kind of feeling?"

"It feels like someone is lightly running their fingers or toes up and down my feet."

I wasn't doing it. And after my experience with funny feelings three years ago, I was more than a little concerned. "Are you sure it's not just a cramp or something?"

"No, it feels so real. I swear someone's tickling me."

Sitting up, I looked at her feet which were propped up on the arm of the couch. Suddenly, I saw some kind of movement near her foot.

"There it goes again," Christy said in frustration, jerking her foot off the couch.

Jumping up, I peered over the end of the couch. "Ah ha, I caught you, you little foot tickler, you."

I grabbed a giggling Megan and pulled her down on top of me. Tickling her, I said, "What are you doing out of bed"

Her face turned serious. "I wov you, Daddy."

"I love you, too, baby girl."

The three of us snuggled down on the couch. Megan was out cold in a couple of minutes. Christy and I weren't far behind her.

*I love my life*, I thought as I drifted off to sleep.

Layne Walker lives in Lake Havasu City, AZ, where he enjoys exploring the desert, dancing, and writing. He began his writing career in the summer of 2010 when he was challenged to write his own novel after years of being an avid novel reader. Once the writing fever got hold of him, he found himself on the adventure of his own life, constantly filled with new ideas for more novels, more action, more fun, and more surprises yet to come. To find out more, visit his website at www.laynewalkerbooks.com.